Mary Wilder Tileston

Sursum Corda

Hymns of Comfort. Third Edition

Mary Wilder Tileston

Sursum Corda
Hymns of Comfort. Third Edition

ISBN/EAN: 9783337081713

Printed in Europe, USA, Canada, Australia, Japan

Cover: Foto ©Andreas Hilbeck / pixelio.de

More available books at **www.hansebooks.com**

Sursum Corda.

HYMNS OF COMFORT.

COMPILED BY THE EDITOR OF

"QUIET HOURS," "SUNSHINE IN THE SOUL," ETC.

Third Edition.

" ABIDE with me! fast falls the eventide;
The darkness deepens; Lord, with me abide!
When other helpers fail, and comforts flee,
Help of the helpless, oh, abide with me."

HENRY F. LYTE.

BOSTON:
ROBERTS BROTHERS.
1891.

Cambridge:
Press *of John Wilson & Son*

Preface.

————•◦•————

THIS volume is intended for all who need comfort and strength, and especially for invalids. I have thought it best to include some of the familiar and cherished old hymns, as well as a large number which are not in the common collections. In many cases, I have given a portion of the hymn instead of the whole. As it was desirable not to make the book too heavy for an invalid to handle, and at the same time to have the type as large as practicable, I preferred to give only the verses which would be most suitable for the special purpose of the book.

These songs of the soul range from the Greek Church of the eighth century to the present day, including the devout lyrics of the seventeenth and eighteenth centuries from "Lyra Germanica," the quaint and earnest words of George Herbert, the glowing utterances of Charles Wesley, Madame Guyon, and Tersteegen, and the fervent and beautiful poems of men and women who still live among us.

It gives me pleasure to express my thanks to the authors who have kindly allowed me to print their poems here ; and also to the publishers — Messrs. J. R. OSGOOD & CO., E. P. DUTTON & CO., HURD & HOUGHTON, D. APPLETON & CO., and ROBERTS BROTHERS — for their permission to use copyrighted poems.

M W. T.

SEPTEMBER, 1877.

Contents.

———◦◦◦———

A Chant.

"Benedictus qui venit in nomine Domini."

I.

WHO is the Angel that cometh?
    Life!
Let us not question what he brings,
    Peace or Strife;
Under the shade of his mighty wings,
    One by one,
  Are his secrets told;
    One by one,
Lit by the rays of each morning sun,
  Shall a new flower its petals unfold,
  With the mystery hid in its heart of gold.
We will arise and go forth to greet him,
Singing gladly, with one accord, —
  "Blessed is he that cometh
    In the name of the Lord!"

II.

Who is the Angel that cometh?
    Joy!
Look at his glittering rainbow wings, —
    No alloy

Lies in the radiant gifts he brings ;
     Tender and sweet,
  He is come to-day,
     Tender and sweet :
While chains of love on his silver feet
  Will hold him in lingering fond delay.
   But greet him quickly, he will not stay,
Soon he will leave us ; but though for others
All his brightest treasures are stored, —
   "Blessed is he that cometh
     In the name of the Lord ! "

III.

Who is the Angel that cometh ?
     Pain !
Let us arise and go forth to greet him ;
     Not in vain
Is the summons come for us to meet him ;
     He will stay,
  And darken our sun ;
     He will stay
A desolate night, a weary day.
  Since in that shadow our work is done,
  And in that shadow our crowns are won,
Let us say still, while his bitter chalice
Slowly into our hearts is poured, —
   "Blessed is he that cometh
     In the name of the Lord ! "

IV.

Who is the Angel that cometh?
    Death!
But do not shudder and do not fear;
    Hold your breath,
For a kingly presence is drawing near.
    Cold and bright
  Is his flashing steel,
    Cold and bright
The smile that comes like a starry light
  To calm the terror and grief we feel;
  He comes to help and to save and heal:
Then let us, baring our hearts and kneeling,
Sing, while we wait this Angel's sword, —
  " Blessed is he that cometh
    In the name of the Lord!"

ADELAIDE A. PROCTER.

Out of the Depths.

A PRAYER IN MENTAL CONFLICT.

MY God! lo, here before Thy face
　　I cast me in the dust;
Where is the hope of happier days?
　　Where is my wonted trust?
Where are the sunny hours I had
　　Ere of Thy light bereft?
Vanished is all that made me glad,
　　My pain alone is left.

I shrink with fear and sore alarm
　　When threatening ills I see,
As in mine hour of need Thine arm
　　No more could shelter me;
As though Thou couldst not see the grief
　　That makes my courage quail,
As though Thou wouldst not send relief
　　When human helpers fail.

O Father, compass me about
 With love, for I am weak ;
Forgive, forgive my sinful doubt,
 Thy pitying glance I seek ;
For torn and anguished is my heart,
 Thou seest it, my God ;
Oh ! soothe my conscience' bitter smart,
 Lift off my sorrows' load.

I know that I am in Thy hands,
 Whose thoughts are peace toward **me** ,
That ever sure Thy counsel stands, —
 Could I but build on Thee !
Though mountains crumble into **dust**,
 Thy covenant standeth fast :
Who follows Thee in pious trust
 Shall reach the goal at last.

Take courage, then, my soul, nor steep
 Thy days and nights in tears,
Soon shalt thou cease to mourn and weep,
 Though dark are now thy fears.
He comes, He comes, the Strong to save ;
 He comes, nor tarries more ;
His light is breaking o'er the wave,
 The clouds and storms are o'er.

DREWES, 1797
Tr. by CATHARINE WINKWORTH.

A CRY FOR HELP.

THOU, infinite in love !
  Guide this bewildered mind,
Which, like the trembling dove,
  No resting-place can find
On the wild waters : God of light,
Through the thick darkness lead me right !

Bid the fierce conflict cease,
  And fear and anguish fly ;
Let there again be peace,
  As in the days gone by ;
In Jesus' name, I cry to Thee,
Remembering Gethsemane !

Fain would earth's true and dear
  Save me in this dark hour ;
And art not Thou more near ?
  Art Thou not love and power ?
Vain is the help of man, — but Thou
Canst send deliverance even now.

Though, through the future's shade,
  Pale phantoms I descry,
Let me not shrink dismayed,
  But ever feel Thee nigh :
There may be grief and pain and care,
But, O my Father, Thou art there !

SARAH E. MILES.

PRAYER FOR STRENGTH.

FATHER, before Thy footstool kneeling,
　　Once more my heart goes up to Thee,
For aid, for strength, to Thee appealing,
　　Thou who alone canst succor me.

Hear me! for heart and flesh are failing,
　　My spirit yielding in the strife;
And anguish, wild as unavailing,
　　Sweeps in a flood across my life.

Help me to stem the tide of sorrow;
　　Help me to bear Thy chastening rod;
Give me endurance; let me borrow
　　Strength from Thy promise, O my God!

Not mine the grief which words may lighten;
　　Not mine the tears of common woe:
The pang with which my heart-strings tighten,
　　Only the All-seeing One may know.

And I am weak; my feeble spirit
　　Shrinks from life's task in wild dismay:
Yet not that Thou that task wouldst spare it,
　　My Father, do I dare to pray.

Into my soul Thy might infusing,
  Strengthening my spirit by Thine own,
Help me, all other aid refusing,
  To cling to Thee, and Thee alone.

And oh! in my exceeding weakness,
  Make Thy strength perfect; Thou art strong:
Aid me to do Thy will with meekness, —
  Thou, to whom all my powers belong.

Oh! let me feel that Thou art near me;
  Close to Thy side, I shall not fear:
Hear me, O Strength of Israel, hear me;
  Sustain and aid! in mercy hear.

ANONYMOUS.

UNCERTAINTY.

O FATHER, hear!
  The way is dark, and I would fain discern
What steps to take, into which path to turn;
  Oh! make it clear.

  My faith is weak;
I long to hear Thee say, " This is the way;
Walk in it, fainting soul; I'll be thy stay;"
  Speak, Lord, oh, speak!

Let Thy strong arm
Reach through the gloom for me to lean upon,
And with a willing heart I'll journey on,
    And fear no harm.

    I wait for Thee
As those who, watching, wait the coming dawn,
Pant, as for water pants the thirsty fawn;
    Oh! come to me.

    It is Thy child,
Who sits in dim uncertainty and doubt,
Waiting and longing till the light shine out
    Upon the wild.

    My Father, see
I trust the faithfulness displayed of old,
I trust the love that never can grow cold, —
    I trust in Thee.

    And Thou wilt guide;
For Thou hast promised never to forsake
The soul, that Thee its confidence doth make;
    I've none beside.

    Thou knowest me;
Thou knowest how I now in darkness grope;
And oh! Thou knowest that my only hope
    Is found in Thee.

CHRISTIAN INTELLIGENCER

THE HOUR OF DARKNESS.

HOW long, O Lord, how long
   Shall on my spirit rest
This weight of darkness and distress?
   How long unto my burning lips be pressed
This overflowing cup of bitterness?
O God, my God! only Thine arm hath power
To bear me through the anguish of this hour.

How long, O Lord, how long!
   Many to rest have gone;
The lovely and beloved are with Thee
   In peace and glory, — while I faint alone
Beneath this burden of mortality.
Yet not alone, — art Thou not near? I bend,
Praying for strength enduring to the end.

How long, O Lord, how long!
   I bow me to Thy will,
Believing in tender love Thou dost chastise, —
   Say to my heart's wild throbbings, Peace! be still!
Father, to Thee, to Thee I lift mine eyes!
Is not Thy smile to patient sufferance given,
Gilding earth's darkness with a gleam of heaven?

How long, O Lord, how long!
   A soft still voice I hear,

Speaking to my worn spirit words of life, —
  "O thou of little faith, how canst thou fear?
I, even I, am with thee through the strife.
Weeping and grief endure but for a night;
The morning breaketh in celestial light."

Sarah E. Miles.

BENEATH THINE HAMMER.

BENEATH Thine hammer, Lord, I lie
    With contrite anguish prone;
Oh, mould me till to self I die,
    And live to Thee alone!

With frequent disappointments sore,
    And many a bitter pain,
Thou laborest at my being's core
    Till I be formed again.

Smite, Lord! Thine hammer's needful wound
    My baffled hopes confess;
Thine anvil is the sense profound
    Of mine own nothingness.

Smite, till from all its idols free,
    And filled with love divine,
My heart shall know no good but Thee,
    And have no will but Thine.

Frederic H. Hedge.

MY GOD, REMEMBER ME!

OH, from these visions dark and drear,
   Kind Father, set me free!
I struggle yet with darkness here, —
   My God, remember me!

Some cheering ray of hope impart,
   Sweet influence from Thee;
And raise this feeble, drooping heart, —
   My God, remember me!

For the inheritance in light,
   On trembling wings I flee,
With sins and doubts and fears I fight, —
   My God, remember me!

BARTRUM.

I LAY my head upon Thy Infinite heart,
   I hide beneath the shelter of Thy wing;
Pursued, and tempted, helpless, I must cling
To Thee, my Father: bid me not depart,
For sin and death pursue, and life is where Thou art!

ANONYMOUS

UNDER A HEAVY PRIVATE CROSS OR
BEREAVEMENT.

O FAITHFUL God! O pitying Heart,
    Whose goodness hath no end;
I know this cross with all its smart
    Thy hand alone doth send!
Yes, Lord, I know it is Thy love,
Not wrath or hatred bids me prove
    The load 'neath which I bend.

Yet, Father, each fresh aching heart
    Will question in its woe,
If Thou canst send such bitter smart,
    And yet no anger know?
How long the hours beneath the cross!
How hard to learn that love and loss
    From one sole Fountain flow!

But what I cannot, Thou true Good,
    Oh, work Thyself in me;
Nor ever let my trials' flood
    O'erwhelm my faith in Thee;
Keep me from every murmur, Lord,
And make me steadfast in Thy word,
    My tower of refuge be!

If I am weak, Thy tender care
Help me to face each ill!

With ceaseless cries and tears and prayer
  The long sad hours I'll fill ;
The heart that yet can hope and trust,
And cry to Thee, though from the dust,
  Is all unconquered still !

PAUL GERHARDT. 1606-1676.
Tr. by CATHARINE WINKWORTH.

THE PENITENT.

O MY God, my Father ! hear,
  And help me to believe ;
Weak and weary I draw near,
  Thy child, O God ! receive.
I so oft have gone astray ;
To the perfect Guide I flee ;
Thou wilt turn me not away,
  Thy love is pledged to me !

I no other claim can bring
  But that I need Thine aid ;
Simply to Thy love I cling,
  On that my hope is stayed.
Thou canst save me, and Thou wilt ;
From my bondage set me free,
Cleanse me from sin's power and guilt ;
  Thy strength is pledged to me !

HYMNS OF THE SPIRIT.

CAST THY BURDEN UPON THE LORD.

THOU! who art touched with feeling of our woes,
 Let me on Thee my heavy burden cast!
My aching, anguished heart on Thee repose,
 Leaving with Thee the sad, mysterious past;
Let me submissive bow, and kiss the rod;
Let me "be still, and know that Thou art God."

Why should my harassed, agitated mind
 Go round and round this terrible event?
Striving in vain some brighter side to find,
 Some cause why all this anguish has been sent?
Do I indeed that sacred truth believe,
Thou dost not willingly afflict and grieve?

My lovely gourd is withered in an hour!
 I droop, I faint beneath the scorching sun;
My Shepherd, lead me to some sheltering bower,
 There, where Thy little flock "lie down at noon:"
Though of my dearest earthly joy bereft,
Thou art my portion still, — Thou, Thou, my God art
  left.

CHARLOTTE ELLIOTT.

PRAYER IN GRIEF.

TO Thee, my God, whose presence fills
  The earth, and seas, and skies,
To Thee, whose name, whose heart is love,
  With all my powers I rise.

Troubles in long succession roll ;
  Wave rushes upon wave ;
Pity, oh, pity my distress !
  Thy child, Thy suppliant, save !

Oh, bid the roaring tempest cease ;
  Or give me strength to bear
Whate'er Thy holy will appoints,
  And save me from despair !

To Thee, my God, alone I look,
  On Thee alone confide ;
Thou never hast deceived the soul
  That on Thy grace relied.

Though oft Thy ways are wrapped in clouds
  Mysterious and unknown,
Truth, righteousness, and mercy stand
  The pillars of Thy throne.

THOMAS GIBBONS. 1784

2

O THOU, FROM WHOM ALL GOODNESS FLOWS.

O THOU, from whom all goodness flows,
   I lift my soul to Thee ;
In all my sorrows, conflicts, woes,
   Dear Lord, remember me !

When on my aching, burdened heart
   My sins lie heavily,
My pardon speak, new peace impart,
   In love remember me !

Temptations sore obstruct my way,
   And ills I cannot flee :
Oh, give me strength, Lord, as my day,
   For good remember me !

Distressed in pain, disease, and grief,
   This feeble body see !
Grant patience, rest, and kind relief,
   Hear, and remember me !

When in the solemn hour of death,
   I lift my soul to Thee,
Be this the prayer of my last breath, —
   Good Lord, remember me !

THOMAS HAWEIS. 1792.

LAMENTATION OF A SINNER.

O LORD, turn not Thy face away
　　From him that lies prostrate,
Lamenting sore his sinful life,
　　Before Thy mercy-gate, —

Which Thou dost open wide to those
　　Who do lament their sin;
Oh, shut it not against me, Lord,
　　But let me enter in.

I need not to confess my life;
　　For surely Thou canst tell
What I have been, and what I am
　　Thou knowest very well.

Wherefore, to beg and to entreat,
　　With tears I come to Thee,
As children that have done amiss
　　Fall at their father's knee.

O Lord, I need not to repeat
　　What I do beg and crave;
For Thou dost know before I ask
　　The thing that I would have.

Mercy, good Lord, mercy I ask,
   This is the total sum :
For mercy, Lord, is all my suit ;
   Oh, let Thy mercy come !

JOHN MARDLEY. 1562.

THE FORGIVENESS OF GOD.

O FATHER ! I have sinnéd. I have done
   The thing I thought I never more should do.
My days were set before me, light all through,
But I have made them dark, — alas! too true, —
And drawn dense clouds between me and my Sun.

Forgive me not, for grievous is my sin ;
Yea, very deep and dark. Alas, I see
Such blackness in it, that I may not be
Forgiven of myself, — how, then, of Thee ? —
Vile, vile without ; black, utter black within !

If my shut eyes should dare their lids to part,
I know how they must quail beneath the blaze
Of Thy Love's greatness. No, I dare not raise
One prayer, to look aloft, lest it should gaze
On such forgiveness as would break my heart !

HENRY SEPTIMUS SUTTON. 1854.

PSALM CXXX.

FROM the depths of grief and fear,
  O Lord! to Thee my soul repairs:
From Thy heaven bow down Thine ear;
  Let Thy mercy meet my prayers.
      Oh, if Thou mark'st
        What's done amiss,
      What soul so pure
        Can see Thy bliss?

But with Thee sweet mercy stands,
  Sealing pardons, working fear:
Wait my soul, wait on His hands;
  Wait mine eye, oh, wait mine ear!
      If He His eye
        Or tongue affords,
      Watch all His looks,
        Catch all His words.

As a watchman waits for day,
  And looks for light, and looks again;
When the night grows old and gray,
  To be relieved he calls amain;
      So look, so wait,
        So long mine eyes,
      To see my Lord,
        My Sun arise.

PHINEAS FLETCHER 1584-1650

LEVAVI OCULOS.

IN trouble for my sin, I cried to God, —
   To the Great God who dwelleth in the deeps.
The deeps return not any voice or sign.

But with my soul I know Thee, O Great God;
The soul Thou givest knoweth Thee, Great God;
And with my soul I sorrow for my sin;

Full sure I am there is no joy in sin;
Joy-scented peace is trampled under foot,
Like a white growing blossom into mud.

Sin is established subtly in the heart
As a disease; like a magician foul
Ruleth the better thoughts against their will.

Only the rays of God can cure the heart,
Purge it of evil: there's no other way
Except to turn with the whole heart to God.

In heavenly sunlight live no shades of fear;
The soul there, busy or at rest, hath peace;
And music floweth from the various world.

The Lord is great and good, and is our God.
There needeth not a word but only these;
Our God is good, our God is great.   'Tis well!

All things are ever God's ; the shows of things
Are of men's fantasy, and warped with sin ;
God, and the things of God, immutable.

O great good God, my prayer is to neglect
The shows of fantasy, and turn myself
To Thy unfenced, unmeasured warmth and light !

Then were all shows of things a part of truth :
Then were my soul, if busy or at rest,
Residing in the house of perfect peace !

WILLIAM ALLINGHAM.

PSALM LVII.

O THOU from whom all mercy springs,
    Compassionate my sufferings,
       And pity me,
       That trust in Thee !
Oh, shelter with Thy shady wings,
   Until these stormes of woe
   Cleare up, or overblow.

GEORGE SANDYS. 1577-1643

FATHER, I HAVE SINNED.

LOVE for all! and can it be?
  Can I hope it is for me?
I, who strayed so long ago,
Strayed so far, and fell so low?

I, the disobedient child,
Wayward, passionate, and wild;
I, who left my Father's home
In forbidden ways to roam!

I, who spurned His loving hold;
I, who would not be controlled;
I, who would not hear His call;
I, the wilful prodigal.

To my Father can I go? —
At His feet myself I'll throw:
In His house there yet may be
Place, a servant's place, for me.

See, my Father waiting stands;
See, He reaches out His hands:
God is love! I know, I see,
There is love for me, — even me!

SAMUEL LONGFELLOW.

GOD'S SURE HELP IN SORROW.

L EAVE all to God,
Forsaken one, and stay thy tears;
For the Highest knows thy pain,
Sees thy sufferings and thy fears;
Thou shalt not wait His help in vain;
Leave all to God.

Be still and trust!
For His strokes are strokes of love,
Thou must for thy profit bear;
He thy filial fear would move,
Trust thy Father's loving care,
Be still and trust!

Know, God is near!
Though thou think Him far away,
Though His mercy long have slept,
He will come and not delay,
When His child enough hath wept,
For God is near!

Oh, teach Him not
When and how to hear thy prayers;
Never doth our God forget;
He the cross who longest bears
Finds his sorrows' bounds are set;
Then teach Him not.

If thou love Him,
Walking truly in His ways,
  Then no trouble, cross, or death
E'er shall silence faith and praise ;
  All things serve thee here beneath,
If thou love God.

ANTON ULRICH, Duke of Brunswick. 1667
Tr. by CATHARINE WINKWORTH.

DEAR REFUGE OF MY WEARY SOUL.

DEAR refuge of my weary soul,
  On Thee, when sorrows rise, —
On Thee, when waves of trouble roll,
  My fainting hope relies.

To Thee I tell each rising grief,
  For Thou alone canst heal ;
Thy word can bring a sweet relief
  For every pain I feel.

But oh ! when gloomy doubts prevail,
  I fear to call Thee mine ;
The springs of comfort seem to fail,
  And all my hopes decline.

Yet, gracious God, where shall I flee ?
  Thou art my only trust ;
And still my soul would cleave to Thee,
  Though prostrate in the dust.

ANNE STEELE. 1716-1778.

PRAYER FOR HELP.

FATHER, help conquer!
    My spirit is sinking,
Deep waters of sorrow go over my head;
    Weeping and trembling,
    And fearing and shrinking,
I watch for the day, and night cometh instead.
    Bitter the cup
    I am hourly drinking, —
How thorny the path that I hourly tread!

    Father, help conquer!
    Earth holds out her lure,
And mortal affections yearn after the prize:
    Scarcely my heart
    Can the struggle endure;
Scarce can I lift up my tear-blinded eyes.
    Father, my Father,
    Thy promise is sure, —
Speak to my spirit, and bid me arise.

    Father, help conquer!
    There is not an hour
Of sorrow or joy but is ordered by Thee;
    Thou dost cut down
    Who hast planted the flower, —

Tempest or calm at Thy bidding shall be.
   Look on my sorrow,
   And give me the power
Humbly to wait till Thou comfortest me.

   Father, help conquer!
   Lord, turn not away!
See with what power the billows increase!
   Give me Thy love
   For my comfort and stay,
Then shall my trembling and murmuring cease.
   Then shall my spirit
   Grow strong for the fray, —
Then shall my weary heart rest in Thy peace.

   Father, help conquer!
   I cry unto Thee!
Hardly my heart its petitions can frame:
   All is so dark
   And so painful to me,
All I can utter, sometimes, is Thy name.
   Father, help conquer!
   My portion now be;
Though all else should change, be Thou ever the same.

Johann Heinrich Schröder. 1696.

I WILL NOT FEAR.

THY will be done! I will not fear
    The fate provided by Thy love;
Though clouds and darkness shroud me here,
    I know that all is bright above.

The stars of heaven are shining on,
    Though these frail eyes are dimmed with tears;
And, though the hopes of earth be gone,
    Yet are not ours the immortal years?

Father! forgive the heart that clings,
    Thus trembling, to the things of time;
And bid the soul, on angel-wings,
    Ascend into a purer clime.

There shall no doubts disturb its trust,
    No sorrows dim celestial love;
But these afflictions of the dust,
    Like shadows of the night, remove.

That glorious life will well repay
    This life of toil and care and woe;
O Father! joyful on my way,
    To drink Thy bitter cup, I go.

JANE E. ROSCOE. 1832.

THOU KNOWEST, LORD.

THOU knowest, Lord, the weariness and sorrow
    Of the sad heart that comes to Thee for rest ;
Cares of to-day, and burdens for to-morrow,
    Blessings implored, and sins to be confessed :
I come before Thee at Thy gracious word,
And lay them at Thy feet, — Thou knowest, Lord !

Thou knowest all the past, — how long and blindly
    On the dark mountains the lost wanderer strayed ;
How the Good Shepherd followed, and how kindly
    He bore it home, upon His shoulders laid,
And healed the bleeding wounds, and soothed the pain,
And brought back life and hope and strength again.

Thou knowest all the present, — each temptation,
    Each toilsome duty, each foreboding fear ;
All to myself assigned of tribulation,
    Or to beloved ones, than self more dear ;
All pensive memories, as I journey on,
Longings for vanished smiles, and voices gone.

Thou knowest all the future, — gleams of gladness,
    By stormy clouds too quickly overcast ;
Hours of sweet fellowship and parting sadness,
    And the dark river to be crossed at last :
Oh, what could confidence and hope afford
To tread that path but this, — Thou knowest, Lord !

JANE BORTHWICK.

SUBMISSION.

B E still, my soul!—the Lord is on thy side;
  Bear patiently the cross of grief and pain,
Leave to thy God to order and provide,—
  In every change He faithful will remain.

Be still, my soul!—thy God doth undertake
  To guide the future as He has the past:
Thy hope, thy confidence, let nothing shake,
  All now mysterious shall be bright at last.

HYMNS FROM THE LAND OF LUTHER.

N O longer doubt, nor fear, nor grieve,
  Nor on uncertain evils dwell;
Past, present, future, calmly leave
  To Him who will do all things well.

CHARLOTTE ELLIOTT.

R EST, weary heart!
  From all thy silent griefs and secret pain,
Thy profitless regrets and longings vain;
Wisdom and love have ordered all the past,
All shall be blessedness and light at last;
Cast off the cares that have so long oppressed,—
  Rest, sweetly rest!

JANE BORTHWICK. 1859

HUMBLY WAIT.

AND shall I sit alone,
 Oppressed with grief and fear.
To God my Father make my moan,
 And He refuse to hear ?

If He my Father be,
 His pity He will show,
From cruel bondage set me free,
 And inward peace bestow.

If still He silence keep,
 'Tis but my faith to try ;
He knows and feels, whene'er I weep,
 And softens every sigh.

Then will I humbly wait,
 Nor once indulge despair ;
My sins are great, but not so great
 As His compassions are.

BENJAMIN BEDDOME. 1818

Aspiration.

THE LONGING SPIRIT.

MY spirit longeth for Thee,
  Within my troubled breast,
Although I be unworthy
  Of so Divine a Guest.

Of so Divine a Guest
  Unworthy though I be,
Yet has my heart no rest
  Unless it come from Thee.

Unless it come from Thee,
  In vain I look around ;
In all that I can see
  No rest is to be found.

No rest is to be found
  But in Thy blessed love :
Oh, let my wish be crowned,
  And send it from above !

JOHN BYROM. 1773.

3

ABIDE IN ME AND I IN YOU.

THE SOUL'S ANSWER.

THAT mystic word of Thine, O sovereign Lord,
 Is all too pure, too high, too deep for me;
Weary of striving, and with longing faint,
 I breathe it back again in prayer to Thee.

Abide in me, I pray, and I in Thee;
 From this good hour, oh, leave me never more;
Then shall the discord cease, the wound be healed,
 The life-long bleeding of the soul be o'er.

Abide in me; o'ershadow by Thy love
 Each half-formed purpose and dark thought of sin;
Quench, ere it rise, each selfish low desire,
 And keep my soul as Thine, calm and divine.

As some rare perfume in a vase of clay
 Pervades it with a fragrance not its own,
So when Thou dwellest in a mortal soul,
 All heaven's own sweetness seems around it thrown.

The soul alone, like a neglected harp,
 Grows out of tune, and needs that hand divine;
Dwell Thou within it, tune and touch the chords,
 Till every note and string shall answer Thine.

Abide in me; there have been moments blest,
 When I have heard Thy voice and felt Thy power;
Then evil lost its grasp, and passion, hushed,
 Owned the divine enchantment of the hour.

These were but seasons beautiful and rare;
    Abide in me, and they shall ever be;
Fulfil at once thy precept and my prayer, —
    Come and abide in me, and I in thee.

HARRIET BEECHER STOWE

DIVINE LOVE.

O LOVE, I languish at Thy stay;
    I pine for Thee with lingering smart;
Weary and faint through long delay,
    When wilt Thou come into my heart?
From sin and sorrow set me free,
And swallow up my soul in Thee!

Come, O Thou universal Good!
Balm of the wounded conscience, come!
The hungry, dying spirit's food,
    The weary, wandering pilgrim's home;
Haven to take the shipwrecked in,
My everlasting rest from sin!

Be Thou, O Love, whate'er I want;
    Support my feebleness of mind;
Relieve the thirsty soul, the faint
    Revive, illuminate the blind;
The mournful cheer, the drooping lead,
And heal the sick, and raise the dead!

CHARLES WESLEY

MY STRENGTH AND MY HOPE.

MY God, my Strength, my Hope,
  On Thee I cast my care,
With humble confidence look up,
  And know Thou hear'st my prayer.
Give me on Thee to wait,
  Till I can all things do ;
On Thee, Almighty to create,
  Almighty to renew.

I want a sober mind,
  A self-renouncing will,
That tramples down and casts behind
  The baits of pleasing ill :
A soul inured to pain,
  To hardship, grief, and loss ;
Bold to take up, firm to sustain
  The consecrated cross.

I want a heart to pray,
  To pray and never cease,
Never to murmur at Thy stay,
  Or wish my sufferings less :
This blessing above all,
  Always to pray, I want ;
Out of the deep on Thee to call,
  And never, never faint.

I rest upon Thy word ;
   The promise is for me :
My succor and salvation, Lord,
   Shall surely come from Thee.
But let me still abide,
   Nor from my hope remove,
Till Thou my patient spirit guide
   Into Thy perfect Love.

CHARLES WESLEY. 1742.

AS THE HART PANTETH.

AS, panting in the sultry beams,
   The hart desires the cooling streams,
So to Thy presence, Lord, I flee,
So longs my soul, O God, for Thee ;
Athirst to taste Thy living grace,
And see Thy glory, face to face.

Ah, why, by passing clouds oppressed,
Should vexing thoughts distract thy breast?
Turn, turn to Him, in every pain,
Whom suppliants never sought in vain ;
Thy strength in joy's ecstatic day,
Thy hope when joy has passed away.

JOHN BOWDLER. 1783-1815.

NEARER TO THEE.

NEARER, my God, to Thee,
    Nearer to Thee!
E'en though it be a cross
    That raiseth me:
Still all my song would be,
Nearer, my God, to Thee, —
    Nearer to Thee!

Though, like the wanderer,
    The sun gone down,
Darkness be over me,
    My rest a stone;
Yet in my dreams I'd be
Nearer, my God, to Thee, —
    Nearer to Thee!

There let the way appear
    Steps unto heaven;
All that Thou sendest me
    In mercy given;
Angels to beckon me
Nearer, my God, to Thee, —
    Nearer to Thee!

Then with my waking thoughts
  Bright with Thy praise,
Out of my stony griefs
  Bethel I'll raise :
So by my woes to be
Nearer, my God, to Thee, —
  Nearer to Thee !

Or, if on joyful wing,
  Cleaving the sky,
Sun, moon, and stars forgot,
  Upwards I fly ;
Still all my song shall be,
Nearer, my God, to Thee, —
  Nearer to Thee !

SARAH F. ADAMS. 1848.

———•◦•———

OH, let my utter helplessness
  Thy kind compassion move !
I cannot, Lord, from sinning cease
  Till I begin to love.

Peace, righteousness, and joy divine
  Thou dost with love impart ;
That Thou art Love, that Thou art mine,
  Assure my happy heart !

CHARLES WESLEY. 1772.

IN THE NIGHT WATCHES.

'TWAS in the watches of the night
    I thought upon Thy power;
I kept Thy lovely face in sight,
    Amid the darkest hour.

While I lay resting on my bed,
    My thoughts arose on high;
My God, my Life, my Hope, I said,
    Bring Thy salvation nigh.

I strive to mount Thy holy hill,
    And climb the heavenly road;
And Thy right hand upholds me still,
    When I commune with God.

Thy mercy stretches o'er my head
    The shadow of Thy wing;
My heart rejoices in Thine aid,
    And I Thy praises sing.

ISAAC WATTS.

PSALM LXIII.

O GOD, Thou art my God alone;
    Early to Thee my soul shall cry;
A pilgrim in a land unknown,
    A thirsty land whose springs are dry.

Thee, in the watches of the night,
    When I remember on my bed,
Thy presence makes the darkness light,
    Thy guardian wings are round my head.

Better than life itself Thy love,
    Dearer than all beside to me ;
For whom have I in heaven above
    Or what on earth compared to Thee ?

JAMES MONTGOMERY. 1822.

A CRY OF THE SOUL.

"*O Dieu de vérité, pour qui seul je soupire.*"

O GOD of truth, for whom alone I sigh,
    Knit Thou my heart by strong, sweet cords to Thee.
I tire of hearing ; books my patience try.
        Untired to Thee I cry ;
        Thyself my all shalt be.

Lord, be Thou near and cheer my lonely way ;
    With Thy sweet peace my aching bosom fill ;
Scatter my cares and fears ; my griefs allay ;
        And be it mine each day
        To love and please Thee still.

My God ! Thou hearest me ; but clouds obscure
    Even yet Thy perfect radiance, Truth divine !
Oh for the stainless skies, the splendors pure,
        The joys that aye endure,
        Where Thine own glories shine !

From the French of PIERRE CORNEILLE.

THE RETURNING DOVE.

O THOU, in whom the weary find
　　Their late, but permanent repose;
Physician of the sin-sick mind,
　　Relieve my wants, assuage my woes;
And let my soul on Thee be cast,
Till life's fierce tyranny be past.

Loosed from my God, and far removed,
　　Long have I wandered to and fro;
O'er earth in endless circles roved,
　　Nor found whereon to rest below;
Back to my God at last I fly;
For oh, the waters still are high.

Selfish pursuits, and nature's maze,
　　The things of earth, for Thee I leave;
Put forth Thy hand, Thy hand of grace;
　　Into the ark of love receive;
Take this poor fluttering soul to rest,
And lodge it, Father, in Thy breast.

Fill with inviolable peace;
　　'Stablish and keep my settled heart;
In Thee may all my wanderings cease,
　　From Thee no more may I depart:
Thy utmost goodness called to prove,
Loved with an everlasting love!

CHARLES WESLEY.

THE NEW COVENANT.

O GOD, most merciful and true,
　　Thy nature to my soul impart;
'Stablish with me the covenant new,
　　And stamp Thine image on my heart.

Remember, Lord, my sins no more,
　　That them I may no more forget;
But, sunk in guiltless shame, adore,
　　With speechless wonder, at Thy feet.

O'erwhelmed with Thy stupendous grace,
　　I shall not in Thy presence move;
But breathe unutterable praise,
　　And rapturous awe, and silent love.

Then every murmuring thought, and vain,
　　Expires, in sweet confusion lost:
I cannot of my cross complain,—
　　I cannot of my goodness boast.

CHARLES WESLEY.

THOU HIDDEN LOVE OF GOD.

THOU hidden love of God! whose height,
   Whose depth unfathomed, no man knows ·
I see from far Thy beauteous light,
   Inly I sigh for Thy repose.
My heart is pained; nor can it be
At rest, till it finds rest in Thee.

Thy secret voice invites me still
   The sweetness of Thy yoke to prove;
And fain I would, but though my will
   Seem fixed, yet wide my passions rove;
Yet hindrances strew all the way, —
I aim at Thee, yet from Thee stray.

'Tis mercy all, that Thou hast brought
   My mind to seek her peace in Thee!
Yet while I seek, but find Thee not,
   No peace my wandering soul shall see.
Oh, when shall all my wanderings end,
And all my steps to Thee-ward tend?

O Love, Thy sovereign aid impart
   To save me from low-thoughted care;
Chase this self-will through all my heart,
   Through all its latent mazes there;
Make me Thy duteous child, that I
Ceaseless may " Abba, Father," cry!

Each moment draw from earth away
  My heart, that lowly waits Thy call ;
Speak to my inmost soul, and say,
  " I am Thy Love, Thy God, Thy All ! "
To feel Thy power, to hear Thy voice,
To taste Thy love, be all my choice.

GERHARD TERSTEEGEN. 1697-1769.
Tr. by JOHN WESLEY. 1738.

FOR DIVINE STRENGTH.

FATHER, in Thy mysterious presence kneeling,
  Fain would our souls feel all Thy kindling love ;
For we are weak and need some deep revealing
  Of trust and strength and calmness from above.

Lord, we have wandered forth through doubt and sorrow,
  And Thou hast made each step an onward one ;
And we will ever trust each unknown morrow, —
  Thou wilt sustain us till its work is done.

In the heart's depths a peace serene and holy
  Abides ; and when pain seems to have her will,
Or we despair, oh ! may that peace rise slowly,
  Stronger than agony, and we be still.

Now, Father, — now, in Thy dear presence kneeling,
  Our spirits yearn to feel Thy kindling love ;
Now make us strong, — we need Thy deep revealing
  Of trust, and strength, and calmness from above.

SAMUEL JOHNSON

AS PANTS THE HART.

AS pants the hart for cooling streams
  When heated in the chase,
So longs my soul for Thee, O God,
  And Thy refreshing grace.

For Thee, my God, the living God,
  My thirsting soul doth pine ;
Oh, when shall I behold Thy face,
  Thou Majesty Divine !

Why restless, why cast down, my soul ?
  Trust God, who will employ
His aid for Thee, and change these sighs
  To thankful hymns of joy.

Why restless, why cast down, my soul ?
  Hope still, and thou shalt sing
The praise of Him who is thy God,
  Thy health's eternal spring.

TATE AND BRADY.

DIVINE EJACULATION.

FOUNTAIN of Light and living Breath,
  Whose mercies never fail nor fade ;
Fill me with Life that hath no death,
  Fill me with Light that hath no shade ;
    Appoint the remnant of my days
    To see Thy power, and sing Thy praise.

O Thou that sitt'st in Heaven, and seest
  My deeds without, my thoughts within, —
Be Thou my Prince, be Thou my Priest,
  Command my soul, and cure my sin:
    How bitter my afflictions be
    I care not, so I rise to Thee.

What I possess, or what I crave,
  Brings no content, great God, to me,
If what I would, or what I have,
  Be not possest, and blest in Thee:
    What I enjoy, oh, make it mine,
    In making me, that have it, Thine.

When winter-fortunes cloud the brows
  Of summer-friends, — when eyes grow strange;
When plighted faith forgets its vows;
  When earth and all things in it change:
    O Lord, Thy mercies fail me never, —
    Where once Thou lovest, Thou lovest for ever.

                    JOHN QUARLES. 1624-1665

ENTIRE CONSECRATION.

O GOD, what offering shall I give
    To Thee, the Lord of earth and skies?
My spirit, soul, and flesh receive,
  A holy, living sacrifice.
Small as it is, 'tis all my store;
More shouldst Thou have, if I had more.

Now then, my God, Thou hast my soul;
    No longer mine, but Thine I am:
Guard Thou Thine own, possess it whole!
    Cheer it with hope, with love inflame!
Thou hast my spirit; there display
Thy glory to the perfect day.

Thou hast my flesh, Thy hallowed shrine,
    Devoted solely to Thy will:
Here let Thy light for ever shine:
    This house still let Thy presence fill:
O Source of Life, live, dwell, and move
In me, till all my life be love!

Send down Thy likeness from above,
    And let this my adorning be:
Clothe me with wisdom, patience, love,
    With lowliness and purity:
Than gold and pearls more precious far,
And brighter than the morning star.

Lord, arm me with Thy Spirit's might,
    Since I am called by Thy great name,
In Thee let all my thoughts unite,
    Of all my works be Thou the aim:
Thy love attend me all my days,
And my sole business be Thy praise.

Joachim Lange.

THE PEACE OF GOD.

WE ask not, Father, the repose
    Which comes from outward rest,
If we may have through all life's woes
    Thy peace within our breast ; —

That peace which suffers and is strong,
    Trusts where it cannot see,
Deems not the trial way too long,
    But leaves the end with Thee ; —

That peace which through the billows' moan,
    And angry tempests' roar,
Sends forth its calm, unfaltering tone
    Of joy for evermore ; —

That peace which flows serene and deep,
    A river in the soul,
Whose banks a living verdure keep ;
    God's sunshine o'er the whole.

HYMNS OF THE SPIRIT.

SURSUM CORDA.

"LIFT up your hearts!" Yes, I will lift
　　My heart and soul, dear Lord, to Thee,
Who every good and perfect gift
　　Vouchsaf'st so lavishly and free.

All that is best, from Thee comes down
　　On us, with rich and ample store,
Thy bounteous hands our wishes crown
　　With good, increasing more and more.

Then, while I live, with ardent eye,
　　Let me look up to Thee, and learn,
From blessings *here,* to look on high,
　　And purer blessings *there* discern !

All Thou hast given is Thine, then take
　　Me, Thine own gift, for all Thine own,
And teach me every day to make
　　New vows of love to Thee alone !

Lyra Catholica

PRAYER FOR GUIDANCE.

O THOU, to whose all-searching sight
The darkness shineth as the light,
Search, prove my heart, it pants for Thee,
Oh, burst these bonds and set it free!

If in this darksome wild I stray,
Be Thou my light, be Thou my way;
No foes, no violence I fear,
No fraud, while Thou, my God, art near.

When rising floods my soul o'erflow,
When sinks my heart in waves of woe,
O Lord, Thy timely aid impart,
And raise my head, and cheer my heart!

If rough and thorny be the way,
My strength proportion to my day;
Till toil, and grief, and pain shall cease,
Where all is calm, and joy, and peace.

GERHARD TERSTEEGEN. 1731

Sursum Corda.

UP TO THE HILLS.

TO the hills I lift mine eyes,
 To the everlasting hills,
Streaming thence in fresh supplies,
 My soul the Spirit feels.
Faithful soul, pray always ; pray,
 And still in God confide ;
He thy feeble steps shall stay,
 Nor suffer thee to slide.

Neither sin, nor earth, nor hell
 Thy Keeper can surprise ;
Careless slumbers cannot steal
 On His all-seeing eyes ;
He is Israel's sure defence ;
 Israel all His care shall prove ;
Kept by watchful Providence,
 And ever-waking Love.

See the Lord, thy Keeper, stand
 Omnipotently near ;
Lo ! He holds thee by thy hand,
 And banishes thy fear ;
Shadows with His wings thy head ;
 Guards from all impending harms ;
Round thee and beneath are spread
 The everlasting arms.

CHARLES WESLEY.

OH, DRAW ME.

OH, draw me, Father, after Thee!
  So shall I run and never tire;
With gracious words still comfort me;
Be Thou my hope, my sole desire:
Free me from every weight; nor fear
Nor sin can come, if Thou art here.

From all eternity with love
Unchangeable Thou hast me viewed;
Ere knew this beating heart to move,
Thy tender mercies me pursued:
Ever with me may they abide,
And close me in on every side!

In suffering be Thy love my peace,
In weakness be Thy love my power;
And when the storms of life shall cease,
My God, in that important hour,
In death as life be Thou my guide,
And bear me through death's whelming tide.

MORAVIAN

EMPLOYMENT.

IF as a flower doth spread and die,
　　Thou would'st extend me to some good,
Before I were by frosts' extremity
　　　　Nipt in the bud ;

　The sweetness and the praise were Thine ;
　　But the extension and the room,
Which in Thy garland I should fill, were mine,
　　　　At Thy great doom.

　For as Thou dost impart Thy grace,
　　The greater shall our glory be.
The measure of our joys is in this place, ˊ
　　　　The stuff with Thee.

　Let me not languish then, and spend
　　A life as barren to Thy praise
As is the dust, to which that life doth tend,
　　　　But with delays.

　All things are busy ; only I
　　Neither bring honey with the bees,
Nor flowers to make that, nor the husbandry
　　　　To water these.

　I am no link of Thy great chain,
　　But all my company is a weed.
Lord ! place me in Thy concert ; give one strain
　　　　To my poor reed.
　　　　　　　　　GEORGE HERBERT

O LOVE DIVINE.

O LOVE divine, how sweet Thou art!
  When shall I find my willing heart
    All taken up by Thee?
I thirst, I faint, I die to prove
The greatness of redeeming Love,
  The Love of Christ to me.

Stronger His Love than death or hell;
Its riches are unsearchable;
  The first-born sons of light
Desire in vain its depths to see;
They cannot reach the mystery,
  The length, and breadth, and height.

God only knows the Love of God;
Oh that it now were shed abroad
  In this poor stony heart!
For Love I sigh, for Love I pine:
This only portion, Lord, be mine,
  Be mine this better part!

Thy only Love do I require;
Nothing in earth beneath desire,
  Nothing in heaven above;
Let earth, and heaven, and all things go;
Give me Thy only Love to know,
  Give me Thy only Love.

CHARLES WESLEY. 1749.

WHOM BUT THEE.

FROM past regret and present faithlessness,
   From the deep shadow of foreseen distress,
And from the nameless weariness that grows
   As life's long day seems wearing to its close, —

Thou Life within my life, than self more near!
   Thou veilèd Presence infinitely clear!
From all illusive shows of sense I flee
   To find my centre and my rest in Thee.

Below all depths Thy saving mercy lies,
   Through thickest glooms I see Thy light arise,
Above the highest heavens Thou art not found
   More surely than within this earthly round.

Take part with me against these doubts that rise,
   And seek to throne Thee far in distant skies!
Take part with me against this self that dares
   Assume the burden of these sins and cares!

How can I call Thee who art always here —
   How shall I praise Thee who art still most dear —
What may I give Thee save what Thou hast given —
   And whom but Thee have I in earth or heaven?

                ELIZA SCUDDER.

"PEACE LIKE A RIVER."

ISAIAH XLVIII.

GIVE me a heart of calm repose
    Amid the world's loud roar;
A life that like a river flows,
    Along a peaceful shore.

I would roll onward to the deep,
    In brightness, not in foam;
And 'mid earth's noise in stillness keep
    My soul's interior home.

Come, Holy Spirit, hush my heart
    With gentleness divine;
Indwelling peace Thou canst impart,
    Oh, make the blessing mine!

Above the scenes of storm and strife,
    There spreads a region fair;
Give me to live that higher life
    And breathe that purer air.

Allay this feverish, restless mood,
    Arrest life's eager chase,
And quench the thirst for earthly good
    With thy bedewing grace!

Come, Holy Spirit, breathe that peace
    Which flows from pardoned sin;
Then shall my soul her conflict cease,
    And find a heaven within.

ANONYMOUS.

I WANT THE SPIRIT OF POWER WITHIN.

I WANT the spirit of power within,
    Of love, and a healthful mind ;
Of power to conquer inbred sin :
    Of love to Thee and all mankind ;
Of health, that pain and death defies,
Most vigorous when the body dies.

Oh that the Comforter would come !
    Nor visit as a transient guest,
But fix in me His constant home,
    And keep possession of my breast :
And make my soul His loved abode,
The temple of indwelling God !

Come, Holy Ghost, my heart inspire !
    Attest that I am born again ;
Come, and baptize me now with fire,
    Nor let Thy former gifts be vain :
I cannot rest in sins forgiven ;
Where is the earnest of my heaven ?

Where Thy indubitable seal
    That ascertains the kingdom mine ?
The powerful stamp I long to feel,
    The signature of love divine !
Oh, shed it in my heart abroad,
Fulness of love, of heaven, of God.

CHARLES WESLEY.

THEE WILL I LOVE.

THEE will I love, my strength, my tower;
   Thee will I love, my joy, my crown;
Thee will I love with all my power,
  In all Thy works, and Thee alone:
Thee will I love till the pure fire
Fill my whole soul with chaste desire.

Ah! why did I so late Thee know,
  Thee, lovelier than the sons of men!
Ah! why did I no sooner go
  To Thee, the only ease in pain!
Ashamed I sigh, and inly mourn,
That I so late to Thee did turn.

In darkness willingly I strayed:
  I sought Thee, yet from Thee I roved:
Far wide my wandering thoughts were spread,
  Thy creatures more than Thee I loved;
And now, if more at length I see,
'Tis through Thy light, and comes from Thee.

I thank Thee, uncreated Sun,
  That Thy bright beams on me have shined;
I thank Thee, who hast overthrown
  My foes, and healed my wounded mind;
I thank Thee, whose enlivening voice
Bids my freed heart in Thee rejoice.

Uphold me in the doubtful race,
　　Nor suffer me again to stray ;
Strengthen my feet with steady pace
　　Still to press forward in Thy way ;
My soul and flesh, O Lord of might,
Fill, satiate with Thy heavenly light.

Give to mine eyes refreshing tears ;
　　Give to my heart chaste, hallowed fires ;
Give to my soul, with filial fears,
　　The love that all heaven's host inspires,
That all my powers, with all their might,
In Thy sole glory may unite.

Thee will I love, my joy, my crown,
　　Thee will I love, my Lord, my God ;
Thee will I love, beneath Thy frown
　　Or smile, Thy sceptre or Thy rod ;
What though my flesh and heart decay,
Thee shall I love in endless day.

　　　　　　　JOHANN SCHEFFLER. 1657
　　　　　　　Tr. by JOHN WESLEY.

A HEAVENLY SOLITUDE.

LORD, with Thy love my soul illume,
　　And then, though dark be all around,
The inward joy, for outward gloom,
　　May only be the more profound.

The eye of faith may farther see
  Into the depths of love divine ;
Because the eye less strong is free
  From things which dazzling, wildering shine.

The circling gloom may but exclude
  Fond dreams, to brighter seasons known,
And make a heavenly solitude ;
  A happy soul, with God alone.

THOMAS DAVIS. 1864.

OPEN, LORD, MY INWARD EAR.

OPEN, Lord, my inward ear,
    And bid my heart rejoice ;
Bid my quiet spirit hear
    Thy comfortable voice ;
Never in the whirlwind found,
    Or where earthquakes rock the place,
Still and silent is the sound,
    The whisper of Thy grace.

From the world of sin and noise
    And hurry, I withdraw ;
For the small and inward voice
    I wait with humble awe ;
Silent am I now and still,
    Dare not in Thy presence move ;
To my waiting soul reveal
    The secret of Thy love.

CHARLES WESLEY. 1742.

THE SPIRIT OF GOD.

THE FOUNTAIN OF WISDOM AND PURITY.

O GOD, O Spirit, Light of all that live,
    Who dost on us that sit in darkness shine,
Our darkness ever with Thy Light doth strive,
    In vain Thou lurest us with Thy beams divine;
Yet none, O Spirit, from Thine eye can hide,
Gladly will I Thy searching glance abide.

O Breath from out the Eternal Silence, blow
    All softly o'er my spirit's barren ground,
The precious fulness of my God bestow,
    That where erst sin and shame alone were found,
Faith, love, and holy reverence may upspring,
In spirit and in truth to worship God our King.

Oh, let my thoughts, my actions, and my will
    Obedient solely to Thy impulse move,
My heart and senses keep Thou blameless still,
    Fixed and absorbed in God's unuttered love.
Thy praying, teaching, striving, in my heart,
Let me not quench, nor make Thee to depart.

I give myself to Thee, to Thee alone,
    From all else sundered, Thou art ever near;
The creature and myself I all disown,
    Trusting with inmost faith that God is here:
O God, O Spirit, Light of Life, we see
None ever wait in vain, who wait for Thee.

GERHARD TERSTEEGEN. 1697-1769.

I SHALL NOT WANT.

THOU All-sufficient One!
   Who art
The chosen portion of my heart!
 Other rejoicing need I none.
  I can find all in Thee,
  Thou chiefest good to me!
Who has Thee is satisfied ;
Who by Thee doth still abide
Is no more lonely, at Thy side.

To whom Thou dost reveal
   Thy face,
He lives in joy in every place, —
 In every time has what he will.
  Who in his deep heart-ground
  To Thee is firmly bound,
Still and joyful, knows no fear.
Earth costs him no bitter tear, —
Earth grows dim when Thou art near.

O highest joy of joy!
   True rest!
Comfort of every aching breast!
 Whom can earth trouble or annoy,
  Whom Thou art near to bless, —
  Who does Thy love possess?

All I seek for out of Thee
Hindrance to my joy might be,
And diminish peace in me.

Whom Thou dost call Thy child,
      Thine own, —
By all on earth may be unknown,
By all on earth may be reviled ; —
  What then ? if God be his,
  He needs no other bliss.
If I know that I have Thee,
Life and strength and joy may flee,
Griefs may come, — they move not me.

Come, O Thou Blessed One,
      My choice !
Now in Thy light make me rejoice,
Come, fill the soul which Thou hast won.
  Come, take the whole, that I
  To Thee may live and die.
I am Thine, oh, be Thou mine,
Until in yonder life divine
Thy face shall on me fully shine !

Gerhard Tersteegen.

NIL LAUDIBUS NOSTRIS EGES.

OUR praise Thou need'st not, but Thy love,
    Our Father and our Friend,
Would have our prayers thus soar above,
    In blessings to descend.

Thy secret judgments' depths profound
    Still sings the silent night ;
The day upon his golden round
    Thy pity infinite.

The soul lost in astonishment
    Would speechless wonder fill ;
But, in the ravished bosom pent,
    Love cannot all be still.

Feeble and faint, she fain would tell
    Of our great Father's love,
Tempering the ills that with us dwell,
    And pledging good above.

Thither would our best thoughts aspire,
    But chains on us abide ;
Oh, quicken Thou our faint desire,
    And to Thy presence guide!

Isaac Williams. 1839

PRAYER FOR STRONG FAITH.

OH for a faith that will not shrink,
   Though pressed by every foe ;
That will not tremble on the brink
   Of any earthly woe ; —

That will not murmur nor complain
   Beneath the chastening rod,
But, in the hour of grief or pain,
   Will lean upon its God ; —

A faith that shines more bright and clear
   When tempests rage without ;
That when in danger knows no fear,
   In darkness feels no doubt ; —

A faith that keeps the narrow way
   Till life's last hour is fled,
And with a pure and heavenly ray
   Lights up a dying bed.

Lord, give us such a faith as this,
   And then, whate'er may come,
We'll taste e'en here the hallowed bliss
   Of an eternal home.

WILLIAM H. BATHURST. 1831.

Morning and Evening.

DAYSPRING OF ETERNITY.

DAYSPRING of Eternity!
    Dawn on us this morning-tide.
Light from Light's exhaustless sea,
    Now no more Thy radiance hide,
But dispel with glorious might
        All our night.

Let the morning dew of love
    On our sleeping conscience rain;
Gentle comfort from above
    Flow through life's long parchèd plain;
Water daily us Thy flock
        From the rock.

Let the glow of love destroy
    Cold obedience, faintly given;
Wake our hearts to strength and joy
    With the flushing eastern heaven;
Let us truly rise ere yet
        Life hath set.

Von Rosenroth. 1684.

MORNING HYMN.

ONCE more from rest I rise again,
    To greet a day of toil and pain,
      My Heaven-appointed lot;
Unknowing what new grief may be
With this new day in store for me;
      But it shall harm me not
I know full well; my loving God
Will suffer not a hurtful load.

My burden every day is new,
But every day my God is true,
      And all my cares hath borne;
Ere eventide can no man know
What Day hath brought of joy or woe;
      And though it seem each morn
To some new path of suffering call,
With God I can surmount it all.

Since this I know, oh, wherefore sink,
My faithless heart? And why dost shrink
      To take thy load again?
Bear what thou canst, God bears thy lot,
The Lord of All, He stumbleth not;
      Pure blessing shalt thou gain,
If thou with Him right onward go,
Nor fear to tread the path of woe.

ANTON ULRICH, Duke of Brunswick. 1667.

WHEN I AWAKE, I AM STILL WITH THEE.

STILL, still with Thee, when purple morning breaketh,
  When the bird waketh, and the shadows flee ;
Fairer than morning, lovelier than the daylight,
  Dawns the sweet consciousness, I am with Thee !

Alone with Thee, amid the mystic shadows,
  The solemn hush of nature newly born ;
Alone with Thee in breathless adoration,
  In the calm dew and freshness of the morn.

As in the dawning, o'er the waveless ocean,
  The image of the morning-star doth rest,
So in this stillness Thou beholdest only
  Thine image in the waters of my breast.

Still, still with Thee ! as, to each new-born morning,
  A fresh and solemn splendor still is given,
So doth this blessed consciousness, awaking,
  Breathe, each day, nearness unto Thee and Heaven.

When sinks the soul, subdued by toil, to slumber,
  Its closing eye looks up to Thee in prayer ;
Sweet the repose beneath Thy wings o'ershading,
  But sweeter still to wake and find Thee there.

So shall it be at last, in that bright morning,
  When the soul waketh, and life's shadows flee ;
Oh, in that hour, fairer than daylight dawning,
  Shall rise the glorious thought, I am with Thee !

HARRIET BEECHER STOWE.

VESPER HYMN.

THE day is done; the weary day of thought and
    toil is past,
Soft falls the twilight cool and gray on the tired earth
    at last :
By wisest teachers wearied, by gentlest friends oppressed,
In Thee alone, the soul, outworn, refreshment finds and
    rest.

Bend, Gracious Spirit, from above, like these o'erarching
    skies,
And to Thy firmament of Love lift up these longing eyes ;
And, folded by Thy sheltering Hand, in refuge still and
    deep,
Let blessed thoughts from Thee descend, as drop the
    dews of sleep.

And when refreshed the soul once more puts on new
    life and power ;
Oh, let Thine image, Lord, alone, gild the first waking
    hour !
Let that dear Presence dawn and glow, fairer than
    Morn's first ray,
And Thy pure radiance overflow the splendor of the
    day.

So in the hastening even, so in the coming morn,
When deeper slumber shall be given, and fresher life
 be born,
Shine out, true Light ! to guide my way amid that deepening gloom,
And rise, O Morning Star, the first that dayspring to
 illume !

I cannot dread the darkness where Thou wilt watch o'er
 me,
Nor smile to greet the sunrise unless Thy smile I see ;
Creator, Saviour, Comforter ! on Thee my soul is cast ;
At morn, at night, in earth, in heaven, be Thou my
 First and Last !

ELIZA SCUDDER. October, 1874.

EVENING HYMN.

THE shadows of the evening hours
 Fall from the darkening sky ;
Upon the fragrance of the flowers
 The dews of evening lie :
Before Thy throne, O Lord of heaven,
 We kneel at close of day ;
Look on Thy children from on high,
 And hear us while we pray.

The sorrows of Thy servants, Lord,
　　Oh, do not Thou despise;
But let the incense of our prayers
　　Before Thy mercy rise;
The brightness of the coming night
　　Upon the darkness rolls:
With hopes of future glory chase
　　The shadows on our souls.

Slowly the rays of daylight fade;
　　So fade within our heart
The hopes in earthly love and joy,
　　That one by one depart:
Slowly the bright stars, one by one,
　　Within the heavens shine, —
Give us, O Lord, fresh hopes in heaven,
　　And trust in things divine.

Let peace, O Lord, Thy peace, O God,
　　Upon our souls descend;
From midnight fears and perils, Thou
　　Our trembling hearts defend;
Give us a respite from our toil,
　　Calm and subdue our woes;
Through the long day we suffer, Lord,
　　O give us now repose!

ADELAIDE A. PROCTER

NIGHT.

WHAT though downy slumbers flee,
Strangers to my couch and me?
Sleepless, well I know to rest,
Lodged within my Father's breast.

He in these serenest hours
Guides my intellectual powers,
And His Spirit doth diffuse,
Sweeter far than midnight dews,

Lifting all my thoughts above,
On the wings of faith and love;
Blest alternative to me,
Thus to sleep or wake with Thee!

What if death my sleep invade?
Should I be of death afraid?
Whilst encircled by Thine arm,
Death may strike, but cannot harm.

With Thy heavenly presence blest,
Death is life, and labor rest;
Welcome sleep or death to me,
Still secure, for still with Thee!

PHILIP DODDRIDGE. 1755.

ALL'S WELL.

THE day is ended. Ere I sink to sleep
    My weary spirit seeks repose in Thine :
Father ! forgive my trespasses, and keep
     This little life of mine.

With loving-kindness curtain Thou my bed ;
    And cool in rest my burning pilgrim feet ;
Thy pardon be the pillow for my head, —
     So shall my sleep be sweet.

At peace with all the world, dear Lord, and Thee,
    No fears my soul's unwavering faith can shake ;
All's well ! whichever side the grave for me
     The morning light may break !

HARRIET MCEWEN KIMBALL.

MIDNIGHT HYMN.

IN the mid silence of the voiceless night,
    When, chased by airy dreams, the slumbers flee,
Whom in the darkness doth my spirit seek,
     O God, but Thee ?

And if there be a weight upon my breast,
Some vague impression of the day foregone,
Scarce knowing what it is, I fly to Thee,
  And lay it down.

Or if it be the heaviness that comes
In token of anticipated ill,
My bosom takes no heed of what it is,
  Since 'tis Thy will.

For, oh, in spite of past and present care,
Or any thing beside, how joyfully
Passes that silent, solitary hour,
  My God, with Thee!

More tranquil than the stillness of the night,
More peaceful than the silence of that hour,
More blest than any thing, my bosom lies
  Beneath Thy power.

For what is there on earth that I desire
Of all that it can give or take from me,
Or whom in heaven doth my spirit seek,
  O God, but Thee!

    ANONYMOUS. (MS. found in a chest, in an English cottage.)

EVENING HYMN.

I REST beneath the Almighty's shade ;
  My griefs expire, my troubles cease ;
Thou, Lord, on whom my soul is stayed,
  Wilt keep me still in perfect peace.

Wherefore in confidence I close
  My eyes, for Thine are open still ;
My spirit, lulled in calm repose,
  Waits for the counsels of Thy will.

After Thy likeness let me rise,
  If here Thou willest my longer stay ;
Or close in mortal sleep mine eyes,
  To open them in endless day.

               CHARLES WESLEY.

Trust and Peace.

THE MERCIFUL PROVIDENCE OF GOD.

SHALL I not sing praise to Thee,
    Shall I not give thanks, O Lord?
Since for us in all I see
    How Thou keepest watch and ward;
How the truest, tenderest love
    Ever fills Thy heart, my God,
    Helping, cheering, on their road,
All who in Thy service move.
All things else have but their day,
God's love only lasts for aye.

When I sleep my Guardian wakes,
    And revives my wearied mind;
Every morning on me breaks
    With some mark of love most kind;
Had my God not stood my Friend,

Had His countenance not been
Here my guide, I had not seen
Many a trial reach its end.
All things else have but their day,
God's love only lasts for aye.

All my life I still have found,
And I will forget it never,
Every sorrow hath its bound,
And no cross endures for ever.
After all the winter's snows
Comes sweet summer back again ;
Patient souls ne'er wait in vain,
Joy is given for all their woes.
All things else have but their day,
God's love only lasts for aye.

Since, then, neither change nor end
In Thy love can e'er have place,
Father ! I beseech Thee, send
Unto me Thy loving grace.
Help Thy feeble child, and give
Strength to serve Thee day and night,
Loving Thee with all my might,
While on earth I yet must live ;
So shall I when Time is o'er,
Praise and love Thee evermore.

PAUL GERHARDT. 1659.

JOY AFTER SORROW.

COMETH sunshine after rain ;
  After mourning, joy again ;
After heavy, bitter grief
Dawneth surely sweet relief ;
    And my soul, who from her height
    Sank to realms of woe and night,
    Wingeth now to heaven her flight.

None was ever left a prey,
None was ever turned away,
Who had given himself to God,
And on Him had cast his load.
    Who in God his hope hath placed
    Shall not life in pain outwaste,
    Fullest joy he yet shall taste.

Though to-day may not fulfil
All thy hopes, have patience still,
For perchance to-morrow's sun
Sees thy happier days begun ;
    As God willeth, march the hours,

Bringing joy at last in showers,
When whate'er we asked is ours.

Every sorrow, every smart,
That the Eternal Father's heart
Hath appointed me of yore,
Or hath yet for me in store,
   As my life flows on, I'll take
   Calmly, gladly, for His sake,
   No more faithless murmurs make.

I will meet distress and pain,
I will greet e'en Death's dark reign,
I will lay me in the grave,
With a heart still glad and brave ;
   Whom the Strongest doth defend,
   Whom the Highest counts His friend,
   Cannot perish in the end.

PAUL GERHARDT. 1606-1676

O LORD, HOW HAPPY IS THE TIME!

O LORD, how happy is the time
   When in Thy love I rest :
When from my weariness I climb
   E'en to Thy tender breast !
The night of sorrow endeth there,
   Thy rays outshine the sun ;
And in Thy pardon and Thy care
   The heaven of heavens is won.

That is not losing much of life
   Which is not losing Thee ;
Thou art as present in the strife
   As in the victory.
And when life's fiercest storms are sent
   Upon life's wildest sea,
My little bark is confident
   Because it holdeth Thee.

Thou art my strength, on Thee I lean ;
   My heart Thou makest sing,
And to Thy pastures green at length
   Thy chosen flock wilt bring.
To others death seems dark and grim,
   But not, O Lord, to me :
I know Thou ne'er forsakest him
   Who puts his trust in Thee.

Wherefore, how happy is the time
   When in Thy love I rest ;
When from my weariness I climb
   E'en to Thy tender breast !
The night of sorrow endeth there,
   Thy rays outshine the sun ;
And in Thy pardon and Thy care,
   The heaven of heavens is won.

WOLFGANG DESSLER. 1692

FATHER OF LOVE.

FATHER of Love, our Guide and Friend,
    Oh, lead us gently on,
Until life's trial-time shall end,
    And heavenly peace be won !
We know not what the path may be
    As yet by us untrod ;
But we can trust our all to Thee,
    Our Father and our God !

If called, like Abraham's child, to climb
    The hill of sacrifice,
Some angel may be there in time ;
    Deliverance shall arise :
Or, if some darker lot be good,
    Oh, teach us to endure
The sorrow, pain, or solitude,
    That makes the spirit pure !

WILLIAM JOSEPH IRONS. 1853.

THE SECRET OF CONTENT.

BE thou content ; be still before
    His face, at whose right hand doth reign
Fulness of joy for evermore,
    Without whom all thy toil is vain.
He is thy living spring ; thy sun, whose rays
Make glad with life and light thy dreary days.
Be thou content.

In Him is comfort, light, and grace,
   And changeless love beyond our thought;
The sorest pang, the worst disgrace,
   If He is there, shall harm thee not.
He can lift off thy cross, and loose thy bands,
And calm thy fears, — nay, death is in His hands.
             Be thou content.

Or art thou friendless and alone,
   Hast none in whom thou canst confide?
God careth for thee, lonely one,
   Comfort and help will He provide.
He sees thy sorrows and thy hidden grief,
He knoweth when to send thee quick relief;
             Be thou content.

Thy heart's unspoken pain He knows,
   Thy secret sighs He hears full well,
What to none else thou darest disclose,
   To Him thou mayest with boldness tell;
He is not far away, but ever nigh,
And answereth willingly the poor man's cry,
             Be thou content.

Be not o'ermastered by thy pain,
   But cling to God, thou shalt not fall:
The floods sweep over thee in vain,
   Thou yet shalt rise above them all;

For when thy trial seems too hard to bear,
Lo! God, thy King, hath granted all thy prayer :
                Be thou content.

Sayst thou, I know not how or where,
    No help I see where'er I turn?
When of all else we most despair,
    The riches of God's love we learn ;
When thou and I His hand no longer trace,
He leads us forth into a pleasant place.
                Be thou content.

We know for us a rest remains,
    When God will give us sweet release
From earth and all our mortal chains,
    And turn our sufferings into peace.
Sooner or later death will surely come
To end our sorrows, and to take us home.
                Be thou content.

Home to the chosen ones, who here
    Served their Lord faithfully and well,
Who died in peace, without a fear,
    And there in peace for ever dwell ;
The Everlasting is their joy and stay,
The Eternal Word Himself to them doth say,
                Be thou content.

PAUL GERHARDT. 1670.

I, EVEN I, AM HE THAT COMFORTETH YOU.

ISAIAH LI. 12.

SWEET is the solace of Thy love,
  My heavenly Friend, to me,
While through the hidden way of faith
  I journey home with Thee,
Learning by quiet thankfulness
  As a dear child to be.

Though from the shadow of Thy peace
  My feet would often stray,
Thy mercy follows all my steps,
  And will not turn away;
Yea, Thou wilt comfort me at last,
  As none beneath Thee may.

Oft in a dark and lonely place,
  I hush my hastened breath,
To hear the comfortable words
  Thy loving Spirit saith:
And feel my safety in Thy hand
  From every kind of death.

Oh! there is nothing in the world
  To weigh against Thy will;
Even the dark times I dread the most
  Thy covenant fulfil;
And when the pleasant morning dawns
  I find Thee with me still.

Then in the secret of my soul,
  Though hosts my peace invade,
Though through a waste and weary land
  My lonely way be made,
Thou, even Thou, wilt comfort me :
  I need not be afraid.

Still in the solitary place
  I would awhile abide,
Till with the solace of Thy love
  My heart is satisfied ;
And all my hopes of happiness
  Stay calmly at Thy side.

ANNA L. WARING.

THY WAY, NOT MINE.

THY way, not mine, O Lord,
    However dark it be !
Lead me by Thine own hand,
  Choose out the path for me.

Smooth let it be or rough,
  It will be still the best ;
Winding or straight, it leads
  Right onward to Thy rest.

I dare not choose my lot ;
  I would not, if I might ;
Choose Thou for me, my God ;
  So shall I walk aright.

The kingdom that I seek
  Is Thine ; so let the way
That leads to it be Thine ;
  Else I must surely stray.

Take Thou my cup, and it
  With joy or sorrow fill,
As best to Thee may seem ;
  Choose Thou my good and ill ;

Choose Thou for me my friends,
  My sickness or my health ;
Choose Thou my cares for me,
  My poverty or wealth.

Not mine, not mine the choice,
  In things or great or small ;
Be Thou my guide, my strength,
  My wisdom, and my all !

HORATIUS BONAR. 1856.

BEHOLD THE FOWLS OF THE AIR.

THE child leans on its parent's breast,
 Leaves there its cares, and is at rest;
The bird sits singing by his nest,
   And tells aloud
His trust in God, and so is blest
    'Neath every cloud.

He has no store, he sows no seed;
Yet sings aloud, and doth not heed;
By flowing stream or grassy mead
   He sings to shame
Men who forget, in fear of need,
    A Father's name.

The heart that trusts for ever sings,
And feels as light as it had wings;
A well of peace within it springs:
   Come good or ill,
Whate'er to-day, to-morrow, brings,
    It is His will!

ISAAC WILLIAMS. 1842.

THE ETERNAL GOODNESS.

I 'LONG for household voices gone,
 For vanished smiles I long;
But God hath led my dear ones on,
 And He can do no wrong.

I know not what the future hath
. Of marvel or surprise,
Assured alone that life and death
   His mercy underlies.

And if my heart and flesh are weak
   To bear an untried pain,
The bruised reed He will not break,
   But strengthen and sustain.

No offering of my own I have,
   Nor works my faith to prove :
I can but give the gifts He gave,
   And plead His love for love.

And so beside the Silent Sea
   I wait the muffled oar ;
No harm from Him can come to me
   On ocean or on shore.

I know not where His islands lift
   Their fronded palms in air ;
I only know I cannot drift
   Beyond His love and care.

                   JOHN G. WHITTIER.

OUR DAILY BREAD.

DAY by day the manna fell;
    Oh to learn this lesson well!
Still by constant mercy fed,
Give me, Lord, my daily bread.

" Day by day," the promise reads;
Daily strength for daily needs:
Cast foreboding fears away;
Take the manna of to-day.

Lord, my times are in Thy hand;
All my sanguine hopes have planned
To Thy wisdom I resign,
And would make Thy purpose mine.

Thou my daily task shalt give;
Day by day to Thee I live:
So shall added years fulfil,
Not my own, my Father's will.

Oh to live exempt from care,
By the energy of prayer;
Strong in faith, with mind subdued,
Yet elate with gratitude!

                   JOSIAH CONDER. 1836.

"THE LORD IS MY PORTION, SAITH MY SOUL; THEREFORE WILL I HOPE IN HIM."

LAMENTATIONS III. 24.

MY heart is resting, O my God, —
   I will give thanks and sing;
My heart is at the secret source
   Of every precious thing.
Now the frail vessel Thou hast made
   No hand but Thine shall fill;
For the waters of the earth have failed,
   And I am thirsty still.

I thirst for springs of heavenly life,
   And here all day they rise;
I seek the treasure of Thy love,
   And close at hand it lies.
And a new song is in my mouth,
   To long-loved music set:
Glory to Thee for all the grace
   I have not tasted yet.

Glory to Thee for strength withheld,
   For want and weakness known,
And the fear that sends me to Thy breast
   For what is most my own.

There is a certainty of love
   That sets my heart at rest, —
A calm assurance for to-day
   That to be poor is best.

Mine be the reverent, listening love,
   That waits all day on Thee,
With the service of a watchful heart
   Which no one else can see;
The faith that, in a hidden way,
   No other eye may know,
Finds all its daily work prepared,
   And loves to have it so.

                   ANNA L. WARING.

MY TIMES ARE IN THY HAND.

MY times are in Thy hand,
   My God, I wish them there;
My life, my friends, my soul, I leave
   Entirely to Thy care.

My times are in Thy hand,
   Whatever they may be;
Pleasing or painful, dark or bright,
   As best may seem to Thee.

My times are in Thy hand,
   Why should I doubt or fear?
A Father's hand will never cause
   His child a needless tear.

                   ANONYMOUS.

A GERMAN TRUST SONG.

JUST as God leads me, I would go :
I would not ask to choose my way ;
Content with what he will bestow,
Assured he will not let me stray.
So as he leads, my path I make,
And step by step I gladly take,
A child in him confiding.

Just as God leads I am content :
I rest me calmly in His hands ;
That which He has decreed and sent —
That which His will for me commands —
I would that He should all fulfil ;
That I should do His gracious will
In living or in dying.

Just as God leads me I abide
In faith, in hope, in suffering true ;
His strength is ever by my side —
Can aught my hold on Him undo ?
I hold me firm in patience, knowing
That God my life is still bestowing —
The best in kindness sending.

Just as God leads, I onward go,
Oft amid thorns and briers keen ;

God does not yet His guidance show;
But in the end it shall be seen
How, by a loving Father's will,
Faithful and true, He leads me still;
Be this my firm relying.

LAMPERTUS GEDICKE.

LIFE.

I MADE a posy, while the day ran by:
Here will I smell my remnant out, and tie
My life within this band.
But time did beckon to the flowers, and they
By noon most cunningly did steal away,
And withered in my hand.

My hand was next to them, and then my heart;
I took, without more thinking, in good part
Time's gentle admonition;
Who did so sweetly death's sad taste convey,
Making my mind to smell my fatal day,
Yet sugaring the suspicion.

Farewell dear flowers, sweetly your time ye spent,
Fit, while ye lived, for smell or ornament;
And, after death, for cures.
I follow straight without complaints or grief,
Since if my scent be good, I care not if
It be as short as yours.

GEORGE HERBERT.

GOD OF MY LIFE.

GOD of my life, whose gracious power
   Through various deaths my soul hath led,
Or turned aside the fatal hour,
   Or lifted up my sinking head :

In all my ways Thy hand I own,
   Thy ruling Providence I see :
Oh! help me still my course to run,
   And still direct my paths to Thee.

On Thee my helpless soul is cast,
   And looks again Thy grace to prove :
I call to mind the wonders past,
   The countless wonders of Thy love.

Whither, oh! whither should I fly,
   But to my loving Father's breast?
Secure within Thine arms to lie,
   And safe beneath Thy wings to rest!

I have no might to oppose the foe ;
   But everlasting strength is Thine.
Show me the way that I should go,
   Show me the path I should decline.

Which shall I leave, and which pursue?
   Thou only mine Adviser be.
My God, I know not what to do ;
   But, oh! mine eyes are fixed on Thee.

Foolish and impotent and blind,
    Lead me a way I have not known :
Bring me where I my heaven may find, —
    The heaven of loving Thee alone.

Enlarge my heart to make Thee room ;
    Enter, and in me ever stay ;
The crooked then shall straight become ;
    The darkness shall be lost in day.

CHARLES WESLEY. 1740.

PEACE, TROUBLED SOUL.

PEACE, troubled soul! Thou need'st not fear,
    Thy great Protector still is near ;
He who has fed, will feed thee still ;
Be calm and sink into His will ;
Who hears the ravens when they cry
Will all His children's needs supply.

Peace, doubting heart! distrust not God ;
Though dark the valley, steep the way,
Still lean upon His staff and rod,
Still make His providence thy stay :
A sudden calm thy soul shall fill ; —
'Tis God who whispers, Peace, be still !

HYMNS OF THE SPIRIT

THE KINGDOM OF GOD.

I SAY to thee, — do thou repeat
    To the first man thou mayest meet
In lane, highway, or open street, —

That he and we and all men move
Under a canopy of love,
As broad as the blue sky above;

That doubt and trouble, fear and pain,
And anguish, all are shadows vain,
That death itself shall not remain;

That weary deserts we may tread,
A dreary labyrinth may thread,
Through dark ways underground be led;

Yet, if we will one Guide obey,
The dreariest path, the darkest way
Shall issue out in heavenly day;

And we, on divers shores now cast,
Shall meet, our perilous voyage past,
All in our Father's house at last.

And, ere thou leave him, say thou this,
Yet one word more: They only miss
The winning of that final bliss,

Who will not count it true that Love,
Blessing, not cursing, rules above,
And that in it we live and move.

And one thing further make him know, —
That to believe these things are so,
This firm faith never to forego,

Despite of all that seems at strife
With blessing, all with curses rife,
That *this* is blessing, *this* is life.

R. C. Trench.

A THANKSGIVING.

LORD, for the erring thought
    Not into evil wrought ;
Lord, for the wicked will
Betrayed and baffled still ;
For the heart from itself kept,
Our Thanksgiving accept.

For ignorant hopes that were
Broken to our blind prayer ;
For pain, death, sorrow, sent
Unto our chastisement ;
For all loss of seeming good,
Quicken our gratitude !

William D. Howells.

A SONG OF TRUST.

O LOVE Divine, of all that is
  The sweetest still and best,
Fain would I come and rest to-night
  Upon Thy tender breast;

I pray Thee turn me not away,
  For, sinful though I be,
Thou knowest every thing I need,
  And all my need of Thee.

I would not have Thee otherwise
  Than what Thou ever art;
Be still Thyself, and then I know
  We cannot live apart.

But still Thy love will beckon me,
  And still Thy strength will come,
In many ways to bear me up
  And bring me to my home.

And Thou wilt hear the thought I mean,
  And not the words I say;
Wilt hear the thanks among the words
  That only seem to pray;

As if Thou wert not always good,
  As if Thy loving care
Could ever miss me in the midst
  Of this Thy temple fair.

For, if I ever doubted Thee,
  How could I any more !
This very night my tossing bark
  Has reached the happy shore ;

And still, for all my sighs, my heart
  Has sung itself to rest,
O Love Divine, most far and near,
  Upon Thy tender breast.

JOHN W. CHADWICK

IN THEE I TRUST.

IN Thee I place my trust,
  On Thee I calmly rest ;
I know Thee good, I know Thee just,
  And count Thy choice the best.

Whate'er events betide,
  Thy will they all perform ;
Safe in Thy breast my head I hide,
  Nor fear the coming storm.

Let good or ill befall,
  It must be good for me ;
Secure of having Thee in all,
  Of having all in Thee.

HENRY F. LYTE. 1834.

"MY TIMES ARE IN THY HAND."

PSALM XXXI. 15.

FATHER, I know that all my life
    Is portioned out for me,
And the changes that are sure to come,
    I do not fear to see ;
But I ask Thee for a present mind
    Intent on pleasing Thee.

I ask Thee for a thoughtful love,
    Through constant watching wise,
To meet the glad with joyful smiles,
    And to wipe the weeping eyes ;
And a heart at leisure from itself,
    To soothe and sympathize.

I would not have the restless will
    That hurries to and fro,
Seeking for some great thing to do,
    Or secret thing to know ;
I would be treated as a child,
    And guided where I go.

Wherever in the world I am,
    In whatsoe'er estate,
I have a fellowship with hearts
    To keep and cultivate ;
And a work of lowly love to do
    For the Lord on whom I wait.

So I ask Thee for the daily strength,
  To none that ask denied,
And a mind to blend with outward life
  While keeping at Thy side ;
Content to fill a little space,
  If Thou be glorified.

And if some things I do not ask,
  In my cup of blessing be,
I would have my spirit filled the more
  With grateful love to Thee, —
More careful, — not to serve Thee much,
  But to please Thee perfectly.

There are briers besetting every path,
  That call for patient care ;
There is a cross in every lot,
  And an earnest need for prayer ;
But a lowly heart that leans on Thee
  Is happy anywhere.

In a service which Thy will appoints,
  There are no bonds for me ;
For my inmost heart is taught "the truth"
  That makes Thy children "free ;"
And a life of self-renouncing love
  Is a life of liberty.

ANNA L. WARING.

THE WISH OF TO-DAY.

I ASK not now for gold to gild
   With mocking shine a weary frame ;
The yearning of the mind is stilled, —
   I ask not now for Fame.

A rose-cloud, dimly seen above,
   Melting in heaven's blue depths away,
Oh ! sweet, fond dream of human Love !
   For thee I may not pray.

But, bowed in lowliness of mind,
   I make my humble wishes known, —
I only ask a will resigned,
   O Father, to Thine own !

To-day, beneath Thy chastening eye,
   I crave alone for peace and rest ;
Submissive in Thy hand to lie,
   And feel that it is best.

A marvel seems the Universe,
   A miracle our Life and Death ;
A mystery which I cannot pierce,
   Around, above, beneath.

In vain I task my aching brain ;
   In vain the sage's thought I scan ;
I only feel how weak and vain,
   How poor and blind, is man !

And now my spirit sighs for home,
   And longs for light whereby to see,
And, like a weary child, would come,
   O Father, unto Thee !

Though oft, like letters traced on sand,
   My weak resolves have passed away,
In mercy lend Thy helping hand
   Unto my prayer to-day.

JOHN G. WHITTIER.

RECONCILIATION.

COME, O ye sinners, to the Lord,
   In Christ to paradise restored :
His proffered benefits embrace, —
The plenitude of gospel grace : —

The guiltless shame, the sweet distress,
The unutterable tenderness ;
The genuine, meek humility ;
The wonder, why such love to me : —

The o'erwhelming power of saving grace,
The sight that veils the seraph's face ;
The speechless awe that dares not move,
And all the silent heaven of love.

CHARLES WESLEY

A PRAYER FOR REST.

GIVE rest, O God, to me ;
 The power to lean on Thee
 In sweet repose.
Give rest to weary thought,
In trust, in doubt, in aught
Assayed, let truth be sought
 From Him who knows.

Give rest, O God, in action,
To wait on Thy correction,
 Devoid of fear.
Faithful and strong to do,
Hopeful whate'er the view,
Since I have naught to rue
 If Thou art near.

Give rest, O God, in sorrow,
Give peace that need not borrow
 From joys to be,
That always finds Thee nearest,
Thy care and love the clearest,
'Mid loss of things the dearest,
 Can I lose Thee ?

Give rest, O God, from care,
The teasing, hourly snare

Of all my thought.
Why fear that given by Thee?
Why lay the load on me?
Why take the work from Thee,
Since Thou hast wrought?

Give rest, O God, in love;
The thought Thou art above
Brings comfort blest.
We know Thee ever near,
We know there's naught to fear,
We know that now and here
Are peace and rest.

INDEPENDENT.

"HE SHALL GIVE HIS ANGELS CHARGE OVER THEE."

THEY who on the Lord rely
Safely dwell, though danger's nigh;
Lo! His sheltering wings are spread
O'er each faithful servant's head.

When they wake or when they sleep,
Angel guards their vigils keep;
Death and danger may be near,
Faith and Love have nought to fear.

SPIRIT OF THE PSALMS.

THE SMOKING FLAX AND BRUISED REED.

WHEN evening choirs the praises hymned
  In Zion's courts of old,
The High Priest walked his round and trimmed
  The shining lamp of gold ;
And if, perchance, some flame burned low,
  With fresh oil vainly drenched,
He cleansed it from its socket, so
  The smoking flax was quenched.

But Thou, who walkest, Priest Most High !
  Thy golden lamps among,
What things are weak, and near to die,
  Thou makest fresh and strong ;
Thou breathest on the trembling spark,
  That else would soon expire,
And swift it shoots up through the dark
  A brilliant spear of fire.

The shepherd, that to stream and shade
  Withdrew his flock at noon,
On reedy stop soft music made,
  In many a pastoral tune ;
And if, perchance, the reed were crushed,
  It could not more be used, —
Its mellow music marred and hushed,
  He brake it, when so bruised.

But Thou, good Shepherd, who dost feed
    Thy flock in pastures green,
Thou dost not break the bruised reed
    That sorely crushed hath been ;
The heart that dumb in anguish lies,
    Or yields but notes of woe,
Thou dost retune to harmonies
    More rich than angels know !

Lord, once my love was all ablaze,
    But now it burns so dim !
My life was praise, but now my days
    Make a poor, broken hymn ;
Yet ne'er by Thee am I forgot,
    But helped in deepest need :
The smoking flax Thou quenchest not,
    Nor break'st the bruised reed.

FAMILY TREASURY.

LIFE'S ANSWER.

I KNOW not if or dark or bright
    Shall be my lot:
If that wherein my hopes delight
    Be best or not.

It may be mine to drag for years
    Toil's heavy chain :
Or day and night my meat be tears
    On bed of pain.

Dear faces may surround my hearth
    With smiles and glee :
Or I may dwell alone, and mirth
    Be strange to me.

My bark is wafted to the strand
    By breath divine :
And on the helm there rests a hand
    Other than mine.

One who has known in storms to sail
    I have on board :
Above the raving of the gale
    I hear my Lord.

He holds me when the billows smite,
    I shall not fall :
If sharp, 'tis short ; if long, 'tis light ;
    He tempers all.

Safe to the land, — safe to the land,
    The end is this :
And then with Him go hand in hand
    Far into bliss.

HENRY ALFORD.

THE SECRET PLACE OF THE MOST HIGH.

" Thou wilt keep him in perfect peace whose mind is stayed on Thee :
because he trusteth in Thee." — Isa. xxvi. 3.

OH, this is blessing, this is rest !
    Into Thine arms, O Lord, I flee ;
I hide me in Thy faithful breast,
And pour out all my soul to Thee ;
And hushing every adverse sound,
Songs of defence my soul surround,
As if all saints encamped about
One trusting heart pursued by doubt.

And oh, how solemn, yet how sweet,
Their one assured, persuasive strain !
"The Lord of Hosts is thy retreat,
Still in His hand thy times remain, —
And He will prove His right to reign
O'er all things that concern thy heart."
O tenderness, O truth divine !
Lord, I am altogether Thine.
I have bowed down, I need not flee, —
Peace, peace is mine in trusting Thee.

And now I count supremely kind
The rule that once I thought severe ;
And precious to my altered mind
At length Thy least reproofs appear.

Now, to the love that casts out fear
Mercy and truth indeed seem one ;
Why should I hold my ease so dear ?
The work of training must be done.
I must be taught what I would know,
I must be led where I would go,
And all the rest ordained for me,
Till that which is not seen I see
Is to be found in trusting Thee.

ANNA L. WARING.

HYMN OF TRUST.

O LOVE Divine, that stooped to share
    Our sharpest pang, our bitterest tear,
On Thee we cast each earth-born care,
    We smile at pain while Thou art near !

Though long the weary way we tread,
    And sorrow crown each lingering year,
No path we shun, no darkness dread,
    Our hearts still whispering, Thou art near !

When drooping pleasure turns to grief,
    And trembling faith is changed to fear,
The murmuring wind, the quivering leaf,
    Shall softly tell us, Thou art near !

On Thee we fling our burdening woe,
    O Love Divine, for ever dear ;
Content to suffer while we know,
    Living and dying, Thou art near !

O. W. HOLMES.

THE DIVINE WHISPER.

LATE on me, weeping, did this whisper fall :
    "Dear child, there is no need to weep at all!
Why go about to grieve and to despair ?
Why weep now through thy Future's eyes, and bear
In vain to-day to-morrow's load of care ?

"Mine is thy welfare.   Yea, the storms fulfil,
On those who love me, none but my decrees.
Lightning shall not strike thee against my will ;
And I, thy God, can save thee, when I please,
From quaking earth, and the devouring seas.

"Why be so dull, so slow to understand ?
The more thou trustest me, the more will grow
My love ; and thou, a jewel in my hand,
Shalt richer be ; whence thou canst never go
So softly slipping but that I shall know.

"If thou dost seem to fall ; if griefs and pains
And death prevail ; for thee there yet remains
My Love, which sent them, and which surely will
Thee reinstate, where thou shalt thenceforth fill
A place still warmer, and more steadfast still."

"Father!" I said, "I do accept Thy word,
To perfect trust in Thee now am I stirred,
By the dear, gracious saying I have heard:"
And having said thus, fell a peace so deep,
What could I do, dear friends? what do, but weep?

HENRY SEPTIMUS SUTTON. 1854.

PSALM CXXXI.

QUIET, Lord, my froward heart,
 Make me teachable and mild,
Upright, simple, free from art,
 Make me as a weanèd child;
From distrust and envy free,
Pleased with all that pleases Thee.

What Thou shalt to-day provide,
 Let me as a child receive;
What to-morrow may betide,
 Calmly to Thy wisdom leave:
'Tis enough that Thou wilt care;
Why should I the burden bear?

As a little child relies
 On a care beyond his own,
Knows he's neither strong nor wise,
 Fears to stir a step alone;
Let me thus with Thee abide,
As my Father, Guard, and Guide.

JOHN NEWTON. 1779.

S

RESTING IN GOD.

" Rest in the Lord, and wait patiently for Him."

SINCE thy Father's arm sustains thee,
Peaceful be ;
When a chastening hand restrains thee,
It is He.
Know His love in full completeness
Fills the measure of thy weakness ;
If He wound thy spirit sore,
Trust Him more.

Without murmur, uncomplaining,
In His hand
Leave whatever things thou canst not
Understand.
Though the world thy folly spurneth,
From thy faith in pity turneth,
Peace thy inmost soul shall fill,
Lying still.

Like an infant, if thou thinkest
Thou canst stand,
Childlike, proudly pushing back
The offered hand, —
Courage soon is changed to fear,
Strength doth feebleness appear ;
In His love if thou abide,
He will guide.

Fearest sometimes that thy Father
  Hath forgot?
When the clouds around thee gather,
  Doubt Him not.
Always hath the daylight broken, —
Always hath He comfort spoken, —
Better hath He been for years
  Than thy fears.

Therefore, whatsoe'er betideth,
  Night or day, —
Know His love for thee provideth
  Good alway.
Crown of sorrow gladly take,
Grateful wear it for His sake ;
Sweetly bending to His will,
  Lying still.

To His own thy Father giveth
  Daily strength ;
To each troubled soul that liveth,
  Peace at length.
Weakest lambs have largest share
Of this tender Shepherd's care ;
Ask Him not, then, " when ? " or " how ? "
  Only bow.

KARL RUDOLPH HAGENBACH
Tr. by H. A. P.

MY PSALM.

I MOURN no more my vanished years:
   Beneath a tender rain,
An April rain of smiles and tears,
   My heart is young again.

The west winds blow, and, singing low,
   I hear the glad streams run;
The windows of my soul I throw
   Wide open to the sun.

No longer forward nor behind
   I look in hope or fear;
But, grateful, take the good I find, —
   The best of now and here.

I plough no more a desert land,
   To harvest weed and tare;
The manna dropping from God's hand
   Rebukes my painful care.

I break my pilgrim staff, — I lay
   Aside the toiling oar;
The angel sought so far away
   I welcome at my door.

All as God wills, who wisely heeds
   To give or to withhold,
And knoweth more of all my needs
   Than all my prayers have told!

Enough that blessings undeserved
   Have marked my erring track ;—
That wheresoe'er my feet have swerved,
   His chastening turned me back ;—

That more and more a Providence
   Of love is understood,
Making the springs of time and sense
   Sweet with eternal good ;—

That death seems but a covered way,
   Which opens into light,
Wherein no blinded child can stray
   Beyond the Father's sight ;

That care and trial seem at last,
   Through Memory's sunset air,
Like mountain-ranges overpast,
   In purple distance fair ;—

That all the jarring notes of life
   Seem blending in a psalm,
And all the angles of its strife
   Slow rounding into calm.

And so the shadows fall apart,
   And so the west winds play ;
And all the windows of my heart
   I open to the day.

JOHN G. WHITTIER.

THE LOVE OF GOD.

THOU Grace Divine, encircling all,
    A soundless, shoreless sea !
Wherein at last our souls must fall,
    O Love of God most free !

When over dizzy heights we go,
    One soft hand blinds our eyes ;
The other leads us, safe and slow,
    O Love of God most wise !

And though we turn us from Thy face,
    And wander wide and long,
Thou hold'st us still in Thine embrace,
    O Love of God most strong !

The saddened heart, the restless soul,
    The toil-worn frame and mind,
Alike confess Thy sweet control,
    O Love of God most kind !

But not alone Thy care we claim,
    Our wayward steps to win ;
We know Thee by a dearer name,
    O Love of God within !

And filled and quickened by Thy breath,
    Our souls are strong and free
To rise o'er sin and fear and death,
    O Love of God, to Thee !

ELIZA SCUDDER.

"CASTING ALL YOUR CARE UPON HIM;
FOR HE CARETH FOR YOU."

O LORD! how happy should we be
  If we could cast our care on Thee,
If we from self could rest;
And feel at heart that One above,
In perfect wisdom, perfect love,
  Is working for the best.

How far from this our daily life!
How oft disturbed by anxious strife,
  By sudden wild alarms;
Oh, could we but relinquish all
Our earthly props, and simply fall
  On Thine almighty arms!

Could we but kneel and cast our load,
E'en while we pray, upon our God,
  Then rise with lightened cheer;
Sure that the Father, who is nigh
To still the famished ravens' cry,
  Will hear, in that we fear!

We cannot trust Him as we should;
So chafes weak nature's restless mood
  To cast its peace away;
But birds and flowerets round us preach,
All, all the present evil teach
  Sufficient for the day.

Lord, make these faithless hearts of ours
Such lesson learn from birds and flowers ;
   Make them from self to cease ;
Leave all things to a Father's will,
And taste, before Him lying still,
   E'en in affliction, peace.

JOSEPH ANSTICE. 1836.

NINETY-FIRST PSALM.

OH, how safe, how happy he,
   Lord of hosts, who dwells with Thee !
Sheltered 'neath almighty wings,
Guarded by the King of kings !
Thou my hope, my refuge art,
Touch with grace my rebel heart,
Draw me home unto Thy breast,
Give me there eternal rest !

Hark the voice of Love divine !
"Fear not, trembler, thou art Mine !
Fear not, I am at thy side,
Strong to succour, sure to guide.
Call on Me in want or woe,
I will keep thee here below ;
And thy day of conflict past,
Bear thee to Myself at last ! "

SPIRIT OF THE PSALMS.

LOOKING UNTO GOD.

" God's hand in all things, and all things in God's hand."

I LOOK to Thee in every need,
    And never look in vain ;
I feel Thy touch, Eternal Love,
    And all is well again ;
The thought of Thee is mightier far
Than sin and pain and sorrow are.

Discouraged in the work of life,
    Disheartened by its load,
Shamed by its failures or its fears,
    I sink beside the road ; —
But let me only think of Thee,
And then new heart springs up in me.

Thy calmness bends serene above,
    My restlessness to still ;
Around me flows Thy quickening life,
    To nerve my faltering will ;
Thy presence fills my solitude ;
Thy providence turns all to good.

Embosomed deep in Thy dear love,
    Held in Thy law I stand ;
Thy hand in all things I behold,
    And all things in Thy hand ;
Thou leadest me by unsought ways,
And turn'st my mourning into praise.

SAMUEL LONGFELLOW.

PEACE.

THOU art with me, O my Father,
    At early dawn of day ;
It is Thy glory brighteneth
    The upward streaming ray :
It calls me by its loveliness
    To rise and worship Thee :
I feel Thy glorious presence,
    Thy face I may not see.

Thou art with me, O my Father,
    In the changing scenes of life,
In loneliness of spirit,
    And in weariness of strife ;
My sufferings, my comfortings,
    Alternate at Thy will ;
I trust Thee, O my Father ;
    I trust Thee, and am still.

Thou art with me, O my Father,
    In evening's darkening gloom :
When night enshrouds the sleeping earth,
    Thy presence fills my room :
The little stars bring messages
    Of kindness from above ;
I love Thee, O my Father,
    And I feel that Thou art love.

JANE EUPHEMIA SAXBY.

NOT KNOWING.

I KNOW not what shall befall me !
   God hangs a mist o'er my eyes,
And thus each step of my onward path,
He makes new scenes to rise :
And every joy He sends me, comes
As a sweet and glad surprise.

I see not a step before me,
As I tread on another year ;
But the past is in God's keeping,
The future His mercy shall clear ;
And what looks dark in the distance,
May brighten as I draw near.

For perhaps the dreaded future
Is less bitter than I think ;
The Lord may sweeten the waters
Before I stoop to drink ;
Or, if Marah must be Marah,
He will stand beside its brink.

It may be He keeps waiting
Till the coming of my feet
Some gift of such rare blessedness,
Some joy so strangely sweet,
That my lips shall only tremble
With the thanks I cannot speak.

Oh, restful, blissful ignorance !
'Tis blessed not to know ;
It stills me in those mighty arms,
Which will not let me go ;
And hushes my soul to rest,
On the bosom which loves me so.

So I go on, not knowing!
I would not, if I might ;
I would rather walk in the dark with God,
Than go alone in the light ;
I would rather walk with Him by faith,
Than walk alone by sight.

My heart shrinks back from trials
Which the future may disclose,
Yet I never had a sorrow
But what the dear Lord chose ;
So I send the coming tears back,
With the whispered word, " He knows ! "

Mary G. Brainard.

FOLLOWING.

AS God leads me, will I go,
  Nor choose my way.
Let Him choose the joy or woe
  Of every day :
They cannot hurt my soul,
Because in His control :
I leave to Him the whole, —
  His children may.

As God leads me, I am still
  Within His hand:
Though His purpose my self-will
  Doth oft withstand.
Yet I wish that none
But His will be done,
Till the end be won
  That He hath planned.

As God leads, I am content;
  He will take care!
All things by His will are sent
  That I must bear.
To Him I take my fear,
My wishes while I'm here. —
The way will all seem clear,
  When I am there!

As God leads me, it is mine
  To follow Him;
Soon all shall wonderfully shine,
  Which now seems dim.
Fulfilled be His decree!
What He shall choose for me,
That shall my portion be,
  Up to the brim!

LAMPERTUS GEDICKE.

AT ALL TIMES.

O THOU whose bounty fills my cup
   With every blessing meet,
I give Thee thanks for every drop, —
   The bitter and the sweet.

I praise Thee for the desert road,
   And for the river-side ;
For all Thy goodness hath bestowed,
   And all Thy grace denied.

I thank Thee for both smile and frown,
   And for the gain and loss ;
I praise Thee for the future crown,
   And for the present cross.

I thank Thee for the wing of love,
   Which stirred my worldly nest,
And for the stormy clouds that drove
   The flutterer to Thy breast.

I bless Thee for the glad increase,
   And for the waning joy,
And for this strange, this settled peace,
   Which nothing can destroy.

JANE CREWDSON.

YOUR HARPS, YE TREMBLING SAINTS.

YOUR harps, ye trembling saints,
    Down from the willows take ;
Loud to the praise of Love Divine
    Bid every string awake.

Though in a foreign land,
    We are not far from home ;
And nearer to our house above
    We every moment come.

His grace will to the end
    Stronger and brighter shine ,
Nor present things, nor things to come,
    Shall quench the spark divine.

Fastened within the vail,
    Hope be your anchor strong ;
His loving Spirit the sweet gale
    That wafts you smooth along.

Or should the surges rise,
    And peace delay to come,
Blest is the sorrow, kind the storm,
    That drives us nearer home.

When we in darkness walk,
　Nor feel the heavenly flame,
Then is the time to trust our God,
　And rest upon His name.

Soon shall our doubts and fears
　Subside at His control ;
His loving-kindness shall break through
　The midnight of the soul.

No wonder, when His Love
　Pervades your kindling breast,
You wish for ever to retain
　The heart-transporting Guest.

Yet learn, in every state,
　To make His will your own ;
And, when the joys of sense depart,
　To walk by faith alone.

Still on His plighted love
　At all events rely ;
The very hidings of His face
　Shall train thee up to joy.

A. M. Toplady.　1772.

THE PILLAR OF THE CLOUD.

LEAD, kindly Light, amid the encircling gloom,
    Lead Thou me on!
The night is dark, and I am far from home, —
    Lead Thou me on !
Keep Thou my feet ; I do not ask to see
The distant scene, — one step enough for me.

I was not ever thus, nor prayed that Thou
    Shouldst lead me on.
I loved to choose and see my path ; but now
    Lead Thou me on !
I loved the garish day, and, spite of fears,
Pride ruled my will : remember not past years.

So long Thy power hath blest me, sure it still
    Will lead me on,
O'er moor and fen, o'er crag and torrent, till
    The night is gone ;
And with the morn those angel faces smile
Which I have loved long since, and lost awhile !

                JOHN HENRY NEWMAN. 1833.

MY DELIVERER.

I WILL trust again His love, His power,
　　Though I cannot *feel* His hand to-day ;
To His help anew I will betake me,
　　Though His countenance seems turned away !
Though without one smile, one gracious token,
　　Through the flames and floods my path must go,
When the fires subside, the waves pass over,
　　My Deliverer I again shall know.

LANGE.

"TO BE OR NOT TO BE."

INFINITE God ! on Thee I rest,
　　Like infant on its mother's breast ;
Within Thy arms I calmly lie,
Nor ask to live, nor seek to die.

Whate'er Thy love ordains for me
Shall by my spirit welcomed be,
Since only good from Thee can flow
To saint above or child below.

E. C.

CHILDLIKE SUBMISSION.

WHAT pleases God, O pious soul,
　　Accept with joy, though thunders roll
And tempests lower on every side,
Thou knowest nought can thee betide
　　　　But pleases God.

The best will is our Father's will,
And we may rest there calm and still;
Oh! make it hour by hour thine own,
And wish for nought but that alone
　　　　Which pleases God.

What most would profit us He knows,
And ne'er denies aught good to those
Who with their utmost strength pursue
The right, and only care to do
　　　　What pleases God.

And must thou suffer here and there,
Cling but the firmer to His care,
For all things are beneath His sway,
And must in very truth obey
　　　　What pleases God.

PAUL GERHARDT. 1653.
Tr. by CATHARINE WINKWORTH.

PSALM XXIII.

MY Shepherd is the Lord ; I know
   No care or craving need :
He lays me where the green herbs grow
   Along the quiet mead :

He leads me where the waters glide,
   The waters soft and still ;
And homeward He will gently guide
   My wandering heart and will.

He brings me on the righteous path,
   E'en for His Name's dear sake.
What if in vale and shade of Death
   My dreary way I take ?

I fear no ill, for Thou, O God,
   With me for ever art ;
Thy shepherd's staff, Thy guiding rod,
   'Tis they console my heart.

Oh ! nought but love and mercy wait
   Through all my life on me,
And I within my Father's gate
   For long bright years shall be.

PSALTER IN ENGLISH VERSE.

THE PULLEY.

WHEN God at first made man,
 Having a glass of blessings standing by,
"Let us," said He, "pour on him all we can:
Let the world's riches, which dispersed lie,
 Contract into a span."

 So strength first made a way;
Then beauty flowed, then wisdom, honor, pleasure:
When almost all was out, God made a stay,
Perceiving that alone, of all his treasure,
 Rest in the bottom lay.

 "For if I should," said He,
"Bestow this jewel also on my creature,
He would adore my gifts in stead of me,
And rest in Nature, not the God of Nature;
 So both should losers be.

 "Yet let him keep the rest,
But keep them with repining restlessness;
Let him be rich and weary, that at least,
If goodness lead him not, yet weariness
 May toss him to my breast."

GEORGE HERBERT

DECLENSION AND REVIVAL.

"*From Me is thy fruit found.*" HOSEA XIV. 8.

DIE to thy root, sweet flower!
    If God so wills, die even to thy root;
Live there awhile an uncomplaining, mute,
Blank life, with darkness wrapt about thy head,
And fear not for the silence round thee spread.
This is no grave, though thou among the dead
Art counted, but the Hiding-place of Power.
      Die to thy root, sweet flower!

Spring from thy root, sweet flower!
When so God wills, spring even from thy root;
Send through the earth's warm breast a quickened shoot;
Spread to the sunshine, spread unto the shower,
And lift into the sunny air thy dower
Of bloom and odor; life is on the plains,
And, in the woods, a sound of birds and rains
That sing together; lo! the winter's cold
Is past! sweet scents revive, thick buds unfold;
Be thou, too, willing in the Day of Power;
      Spring from thy root, sweet flower!

                    DORA GREENWELL.

TRUE REST.

GOD sends sometimes a stillness in our life,
  The bivouac, the sleep,
When on the silent battle-field the strife
  Is hushed in slumber deep,
When wearied hearts exhausted sink to rest,
Remembering nor the struggle nor the quest.

We know such hours, when the dim dewy night
  Bids day's hot turmoil cease ;
When star by star steals noiselessly in sight,
  With silent smiles of peace ;
When we lay down our load, and half forget
The morrow comes, and we must bear it yet.

We know such hours, when after days of pain,
  And nights when sleep was not,
God gives us ease and peace and calm again,
  Till, all the past forgot,
We say, in rest and thankfulness most deep,
E'en so " He giveth His beloved sleep."

When some strong chain that bound us by God's strength
  Is loosed or torn apart ;
Or when, beloved and longed-for, come at length,
  Some friend makes glad our heart, —
We know the calm that follows on such bliss,
That looks no farther, satisfied with this.

God does not always loose the chain, nor give
    The loved ones back to us ;
Sometimes, 'mid strife and tumult we must live,
    Learning His silence thus :
There is a rest for those who bear His will,
A peacefulness than freedom sweeter still.

He giveth rest more perfect, pure, and true,
    While we His burthen bear ;
It springeth not from parted pain, but through
    The accepted blessing there ;
The lesson pondered o'er with thoughtful eyes,
The faith that sees in all a meaning wise.

Deep in the heart of pain God's hand hath set
    A hidden rest and bliss ;
Take as His gift the pain, the gift brings yet
    A truer happiness :
God's voice speaks, through it all, the high behest
That bids His people enter into rest.

Lucy Fletcher.

COMMIT THOU ALL THY GRIEFS.

COMMIT thou all thy griefs
    And ways into His hands,
To His sure trust and tender care,
    Who earth and heaven commands.

Who points the clouds their course,
Whom winds and seas obey,
He shall direct thy wandering feet,
He shall prepare thy way.

Thou on the Lord rely,
So safe shalt thou go on ;
Fix on His work thy steadfast eye,
So shall thy work be done.

No profit canst thou gain
By self-consuming care ;
To Him commend thy cause ; His ear
Attends the softest prayer.

Thy everlasting Truth,
Father ! Thy ceaseless love,
Sees all Thy children's wants, and knows
What best for each will prove.

Give to the winds thy fears ;
Hope, and be undismayed ;
God hears thy sighs, and counts thy tears,
God shall lift up thy head.

Through waves and clouds and storms,
He gently clears thy way ;
Wait thou His time ; so shall this night
Soon end in joyous day.

Still heavy is thy heart?
Still sink thy spirits down?
Cast off the weight, let fear depart,
And every care be gone.

Thou seest our weakness, Lord!
Our hearts are known to Thee:
Oh! lift Thou up the sinking hand,
Confirm the feeble knee!

Let us in life, in death,
Thy steadfast Truth declare,
And publish, with our latest breath,
Thy love and guardian care!

PAUL GERHARDT.
Tr. by JOHN WESLEY. 1739.

HAPPINESS FOUND.

L ORD, it is not life to live,
   If Thy presence Thou deny;
Lord, if Thou Thy presence give,
   'Tis no longer death to die.
Source and giver of repose,
Singly from Thy smile it flows;
Peace and happiness are Thine;
Mine they are, if Thou art mine.

A. M. TOPLADY.

AWAY, MY NEEDLESS FEARS.

AWAY, my needless fears,
    And doubts no longer mine !
A ray of heavenly light appears,
    A messenger divine.
    Thrice comfortable hope,
    That calms my stormy breast ;
My Father's hand prepares the cup,
    And what He wills is best.

He knows whate'er I want,
    He sees my helplessness,
And always readier is to grant
    Than I to ask His grace.
    My fearful heart He reads,
    Secures my soul from harms,
And underneath His mercy spreads
    Its everlasting arms.

Here is firm footing ; here,
    My soul, is solid rock,
To break the waves of grief and fear,
    And trouble's rudest shock :
    This only can sustain
    When earth and heaven remove :
O turn thee to thy Rest again , —
    Thy God's eternal Love !

CHARLES WESLEY

QUIET FROM GOD.

" When He giveth quietness, who then can make trouble ? "

QUIET from God! how beautiful to keep
 This treasure, the All-merciful hath given ;
To feel, when we awake and when we sleep,
 Its incense round us, like a breath from heaven !

To sojourn in the world, and yet apart ;
 To dwell with God, yet still with man to feel ;
To bear about for ever in the heart
 The gladness which His Spirit doth reveal !

Who shall make trouble ? Not the evil minds
 Which like a shadow o'er creation lower ;
The soul which peace hath thus attunèd finds
 How strong within doth reign the Calmer's power.

What shall make trouble ? Not the holy thought
 Of the departed ; that will be a part
Of those undying things His peace hath wrought
 Into a world of beauty in the heart.

What shall make trouble ? Not slow-wasting pain,
 Not the impending, certain stroke of death ;
These do but wear away, then snap the chain
 Which bound the spirit down to things beneath.

       Sarah J. Williams.

FOR EVER WITH THE LORD.

FOR ever with the Lord !
    Amen ! so let it be !
Life from the dead is in that word,
    And immortality.

Here in the body pent,
    Absent from Him I roam,
Yet nightly pitch my moving tent
    A day's march nearer home.

My Father's house on high,
    Home of my soul ! how near,
At times, to faith's foreseeing eye,
    Thy golden gates appear !

Yet clouds will intervene,
    And all my prospect flies,
Like Noah's dove, I flit between
    Rough seas and stormy skies.

Anon the clouds depart,
    The winds and waters cease,
While sweetly o'er my gladdened heart
    Expands the bow of peace !

Beneath its glowing arch,
    Along the hallowed ground,
I see cherubic armies march,
    A camp of fire around.

I hear at morn and even,
    At noon and midnight hour,
The choral harmonies of heaven
    Earth's Babel tongues o'erpower.

Then, then I feel that He,
    Remembered or forgot,
The Lord, is never far from me,
    Though I perceive Him not.

For ever with the Lord !
    Father, if 'tis Thy will,
The promise of that gracious word,
    E'en here, to me fulfil.

Be Thou at my right hand,
    Then shall I never fail ;
Uphold me, and I needs must stand ;
    Fight, and I shall prevail.

JAMES MONTGOMERY.

REDEMPTION FOUND.

FATHER! Thine everlasting grace
   Our scanty thought surpasses far;
Thy heart is full of tenderness,
   Thy arms of love still open are
Returning sinners to receive,
That mercy they may taste, and live.

Though waves and storms go o'er my head,
   Though strength and health and friends be gone,
Though joys be withered all, and dead,
   Though every comfort be withdrawn,
On this my steadfast soul relies,
Father! Thy mercy never dies.

Fixed on this ground will I remain,
   Though my heart fail and flesh decay;
This anchor shall my soul sustain,
   When earth's foundations melt away;
Mercy's full power I then shall prove,
Loved with an everlasting love.

JOHANN ANDREAS ROTHE. 1728.
Tr. by JOHN WESLEY. 1740.

Submission in Sorrow.

PEACE IN TROUBLE.

WHAT within me and without
    Hourly on my spirit weighs,
Burdening heart and soul with doubt,
    Darkening all my weary days:
In it I behold Thy will,
    God, who givest rest and peace,
And my heart is calm and still,
    Waiting till Thou send release.

When my trials tarry long,
    Unto Thee I look and wait,
Knowing none, though keen and strong,
    Can my faith in Thee abate.
O my soul, why art thou vexed?
    Let things go e'en as they will;
Though to thee they seem perplexed,
    Yet His order they fulfil.

A. H. FRANCKE. 1663-1727

THE QUIET HOPING HEART.

WHATE'ER my God ordains is right,
    His will is ever just;
Howe'er He order now my cause,
  I will be still and trust.
    He is my God;
    Though dark my road,
He holds me that I shall not fall,
Wherefore to Him I leave it all.

Whate'er my God ordains is right,
  Though I the cup must drink
That bitter seems to my faint heart,
  I will not fear nor shrink;
    Tears pass away
    With dawn of day,
Sweet comfort yet shall fill my heart,
And pain and sorrow shall depart.

Whate'er my God ordains is right,
  My Light, my Life is He,
Who cannot will me aught but good,
  I trust Him utterly;
    For well I know,
    In joy or woe,
We soon shall see as sunlight clear
How faithful was our Guardian here.

Whate'er my God ordains is right,
　　Here will I take my stand ;
Through sorrow, need, or death make earth
　　For me a desert land,
　　　　My Father's care
　　　　Is around me there ;
He holds me that I shall not fall,
And so to Him I leave it all.

SAMUEL RODIGAST. 1675.

EASTER-DAY.

THE graves grow thicker, and life's ways more bare,
　　As years on years go by :
Nay ! thou hast more green gardens in thy care,
　　And more stars in thy sky !

Behind, hopes turned to griefs, and joys to memories
　　Are fading out of sight :
Before, pains changed to peace, and dreams to certainties
　　Are glowing in God's Light.

Hither come backslidings, defeats, distresses,
　　Vexing this mortal strife :
Thither go progress, victories, successes,
　　Crowning immortal Life.

No jubilees, few gladsome festive hours
　　Form landmarks for my way :
But Heaven and earth and Saints and friends and flowers
　　Are keeping Easter-Day !

R. E. J. A.　From "Lyra Mystica."

TIRED.

" Does the road wind uphill all the way ? —
Yes, to the very end."

SO tired ! — I fain would rest ;
   But, Lord, Thou knowest best :
   I wait on Thee.
I will toil on from day to day,
Bearing my cross, and only pray
   To follow Thee.

So tired : yet I would work
For Thee ! — Lord, hast Thou work
   Even for me ?
Small things — which others, hurrying on
In Thy blest service, swift and strong,
   Might never see ?

So tired : yet I might reach
A flower, to cheer and teach
   Some sadder heart ;
Or for parched lips perhaps might bring
One cup of water from the spring,
   Ere I depart.

So tired : yet it were sweet
Some faltering tender feet
   To help and guide ;

Thy little ones whose steps are slow,
I should not weary them, I know,
   Nor roughly chide.

So tired! Lord, Thou wilt come
To take me to my home,
   So long desired :
Only Thy grace and mercy send,
That I may serve Thee to the end,
   Though I am tired.

M. E. T.   From " Voices of Comfort."

SONNET ON HIS BLINDNESS.

WHEN I consider how my light is spent,
   Ere half my days, in this dark world and wide,
And that one talent which is death to hide
Lodged with me useless, though my soul more bent
To serve therewith my Maker, and present
My true account, lest he returning chide, —
" Doth God exact day-labor, light denied ? "
I fondly ask ; but Patience, to prevent
That murmur, soon replies : " God doth not need
Either man's work or His own gifts ; who best
Bear His mild yoke, they serve Him best ; His state
Is kingly. Thousands at His bidding speed,
And post o'er land and ocean without rest :
They also serve who only stand and wait."

JOHN MILTON.

THE BLIND ASLEEP.

" I ALWAYS see in dreams," she said,
 " Nor then believe that I am blind."
That simple thought a shadowy pleasure shed
  Within my mind.

In a like doom, the nights afford
 A like display of mercy done.
How oft I've dreamed of sight as full restored !
  Not once as gone.

Restored as with a flash ! I gaze
 On open books with letters plain ;
And scenes and faces of the dearer days
  Are bright again.

O Sleep ! in pity thou art made
 A double boon to such as we ;
Beneath closed lids and folds of deepest shade
  We think we see.

O Providence ! when all is dark
 Around our steps and o'er Thy will,
The mercy-seat that hides the covenant-ark
  Has angels still.

Thou who art light ! illume the page
 Within ; renew these respites sweet,
And show beyond the films and wear of age
  Both walk and seat.

N. L. FROTHINGHAM. 1865

HYMN FOR THE BLIND.

O GOD! to Thine all-seeing ken
   The night and day are one;
The blackness of earth's deepest den,
   And flaming of the sun.

Both lend to eyes of mortal race
   Their sweet and mingled aid;
And blest in its alternate place
   The shining and the shade.

For us, a cloud is on the sight,
   And Nature's face is hid;
Alike untouched by figured light,
   The eyeball and the lid.

So it hath pleased Thee, God!   Be each
   Sore plaint and passion still;
And holy thoughts kneel down, and teach
   Submission to that will.

From all our diminutions, Lord,
   Let trust and love increase;
And all our hindrances reward
   With patience and with peace.

Oh, clear the mind!   Be more and more
   The invisible revealed;
And spirits brighten at the door,
   When all without is sealed!

N. L. Frothingham.   1865.

Submission in Sorrow.

THE DEAF AND THE BLIND.

THE deaf man sees the prison wall
    Of mutes and mimes that hems him round ;
With peering gaze he scans them all,
    His answer is a blank of sound.

The blind man listening walks ; and, when
    The living voices meet his ear,
A world of souls is near him then,
    With inner light his heart to cheer.

The deaf man reads the written signs,
    Where living thoughts their impress trace,
And, oh ! what recognition shines,
    As he looks upward to the face !

The blind man sees not how the ray
    Of morning crimsons all the skies ;
At eve, he sees not how the day
    In soft and tender beauty dies.

Which loses most ? ah ! who shall say ?
    But, deaf and blind at once to be ;
To miss all sight and sound of day, —
    No voice to hear, no face to see !

" Silence and darkness " walk, in song,
    Two " solemn sisters ; " but to him
Who deaf and blind sits all day long,
    Twin jailers are they, stark and grim.

Yet still is left the hand's warm grasp
  That speaks and is so much of bliss!
The tender cheek, the loving clasp,
  The silent language of the kiss!

And so, as one by one expire
  The dear delights of earthly sense,
The soul's deep founts of inner fire
  Gush up with fervor more intense.

O soul! live inward! in thy realm
  Of light and love and loveliness!
Then, though dark fate earth's house may whelm,
  The peace of God thy home shall bless.

CHARLES T. BROOKS.

DISCIPLINE.

TREMBLE not, though darkly gather
  Clouds and tempests o'er thy sky;
Still believe, thy heavenly Father
  Loves thee best when storms are nigh.

Love divine has seen and counted
  Every tear it caused to fall,
And the storm which Love appointed
  Was its choicest gift of all.

JANE BORTHWICK.

TRUST IN GOD.

LEAVE God to order all thy ways,
　　And hope in Him whate'er betide;
Thou'lt find Him in the evil days
　　Thy all-sufficient strength and guide;
Who trusts in God's unchanging love,
Builds on the rock that nought can move.

What can these anxious cares avail,
　　These never-ceasing moans and sighs?
What can it help us to bewail
　　Each painful moment as it flies?
Our cross and trials do but press
The heavier for our bitterness.

Only thy restless heart keep still,
　　And wait in cheerful hope; content
To take whate'er His gracious will,
　　His all-discerning love hath sent.
Doubt not our inmost wants are known
To Him who chose us for His own.

He knows when joyful hours are best,
　　He sends them as He sees it meet;
When thou hast borne the fiery test,
　　And art made free from all deceit,
He comes to thee all unaware,
And makes thee own His loving care.

Sing, pray, and swerve not from His ways,
    But do thine own part faithfully ;
Trust His rich promises of grace,
    So shall they be fulfilled in thee :
God never yet forsook at need
The soul that trusted Him indeed.

GEORG NEUMARCK. 1653.

TRUST IN DIVINE GOODNESS.

MY God! I thank Thee ; may no thought
    E'er deem Thy chastisements severe ;
But may this heart, by sorrow taught,
    Calm each wild wish, each idle fear.

Thy mercy bids all nature bloom ;
    The sun shines bright, and man is gay ;
Thine equal mercy spreads the gloom
    That darkens o'er his little day.

Full many a throb of grief and pain
    Thy frail and erring child must know ;
But not one prayer is breathed in vain,
    Nor does one tear unheeded flow.

Thy various messengers employ !
    Thy purposes of love fulfil !
And, 'mid the wreck of human joy,
    May kneeling faith adore Thy will.

ANDREWS NORTON. 1809.

THE GUEST.

" Behold, I stand at the door, and knock: if any man hear my voice, and open the door, I will come in to him, and will sup with him, and he with me." — REV. iii. 20.

SPEECHLESS Sorrow sat with me ;
 I was sighing wearily !
Lamp and fire were out: the rain
Wildly beat the window-pane.
In the dark we heard a knock,
And a hand was on the lock ;
One in waiting spake to me,
   Saying sweetly,
" *I am come to sup with thee !* "

All my room was dark and damp ;
" Sorrow," said I, " trim the lamp ;
Light the fire, and cheer thy face ;
Set the guest-chair in its place."
And again I heard the knock ;
In the dark I found the lock : —
" Enter ! I have turned the key !
   Enter, Stranger !
Who art come to sup with me."

Opening wide the door he came,
But I could not speak his name ;
In the guest-chair took his place ;
But I could not see his face !

When my cheerful fire was beaming,
When my little lamp was gleaming,
And the feast was spread for three,
    Lo! my MASTER
Was the Guest that supped with me!

HARRIET MCEWEN KIMBALL.

I THANK THEE FOR THE LONELINESS.

I THANK Thee for the loneliness
    That brings me near to Thee; —
Thanks that no other heart can bless,
    No other eye can see!
I never knew the depth, the height,
    Of heavenly love before:
O Lord! Thy presence gilds my night,
    It brightens more and more.

What matter, in that lucid gleam,
    If stars grow bright or pale?
Shall we of lesser glories dream
    Who look within the vail?
Why count the little earthly loss,
    When gifts from Heaven flow down?
Lord, Thou for me hast set the Cross
    With jewels of the Crown.

A. G. R.

DRYNESS IN PRAYER.

OH for the happy days gone by,
  When love ran smooth and free,
Days when my spirit so enjoyed
  More than earth's liberty!

This freezing heart, O Lord! this will
  Dry as the desert sand,
Good thoughts that will not come, bad thoughts
  That come without command : —

If this drear change be Thine, O Lord!
  If it be Thy sweet will, —
Spare not, but to the very brim
  The bitter chalice fill.

But, if it hath been sin of mine,
  Oh, show that sin to me!
Not to get back the sweetness lost,
  But to make peace with Thee.

One thing alone, dear Lord! I dread : —
  To have a secret spot
That separates my soul from Thee,
  And yet to know it not.

But if this weariness hath come
  A present from on high,
Teach me to find the hidden wealth
  That in its depths may lie.

So in this darkness I can learn
   To tremble and adore,
To sound my own vile nothingness,
   And thus to love Thee more, —

To love Thee, and yet not to think
   That I can love so much, —
To have Thee with me, Lord, all day,
   Yet not to feel Thy touch.

Oh, blessed be this darkness then,
   This deep in which I lie;
And blessed be all things that teach
   God's great supremacy!

F. W. FABER.

THE LAST WISH.

TO do, or not to do; to have,
   Or not to have, I leave to Thee;
To be or not to be, I leave;
   Thy only will be done in me.
All my requests are lost in one;
Father, Thy only will be done!

Suffice that for the season past
   Myself in things divine I sought,
For comforts cried with eager haste,
   And murmured when I found them not:
I leave it now to Thee alone;
Father, Thy only will be done!

CHARLES WESLEY. 1749.

DESPONDENCY CORRECTED.

FROM "THE EXCURSION."

ONE adequate support
        For the calamities of mortal life
Exists, one only : an assured belief
That the procession of our fate, howe'er
Sad or disturbed, is ordered by a Being
Of infinite benevolence and power ;
Whose everlasting purposes embrace
All accidents, converting them to good. —
The darts of anguish fix not where the seat
Of suffering hath been thoroughly fortified
By acquiescence in the Will Supreme
For Time and for Eternity ; by faith,
Faith absolute in God, including hope,
And the defence that lies in boundless love
Of His perfections, with habitual dread
Of aught unworthily conceived, endured
Impatiently ; ill-done, or left undone,
To the dishonor of His holy Name.
Soul of our souls, and safeguard of the world !
Sustain — Thou only canst — the sick of heart ;
Restore their languid spirits, and recall
Their lost affections unto Thee and Thine !

WILLIAM WORDSWORTH

REST 'IN GOD.

YEA, my spirit fain would sink
    In Thy heart and hands, my God,
Waiting till Thou show the end
    Of the ways she here hath trod ;
Stripped of self, how calm her rest
    On her loving Father's breast !

And my soul complaineth not ;
    For she knows not pain or fear,
Clinging to her God in faith,
    Trusting though He slay her here.
'Tis when flesh and blood repine,
    Sun of joy, Thou canst not shine.

Thus my soul before her God
    Lieth still, nor speaketh more,
Conqueror thus o'er pain and wrong,
    That once smote her to the core ;
Like a silent ocean, bright
    With her God's great praise and light.

WINKLER. 1713.

CONTENT TO SUFFER.

HOW oft a gleam of glory sent
　　Straight through the deepest, darkest night,
　Has filled the soul with heavenly light,
With holy peace and sweet content !

Content to wait the will of God,
　To cast on Him the heavy load,
　To walk with Him the weary road
With patience, leaning on the Lord.

Content to suffer and be still,
　Without complaining bear the cross,
　Endure the pain, accept the loss
Of all earth's treasures, if God will.

ANONYMOUS.

COUPLETS.

WHEN thou hast thanked thy God for every bless-
　　　ing sent,
What time will then remain for murmurs or lament?

When God afflicts thee, think He hews a rugged stone,
Which must be shaped, or else aside as useless thrown.

R. C. TRENCH.

MEDICINE.

MUSING of all my Father's love,
　　How sweet it is !
Methought I heard a gentle voice :
　　"Child, here's the cup,
I've mixed it, — drink it up."
My heart did sink, — I could no more rejoice.

"O Father, must it be ? " —
　　" Yes, child, it must." —
"Then give the needed medicine ;
　　Be by my side,
Only Thy face don't hide,
I'll drink it all : it must be good, — 'tis Thine."

FROM AN OLD ENGLISH TRACT.

HE GIVETH SONGS IN THE NIGHT.

WE praise Thee oft for hours of bliss,
　　For days of quiet rest :
But, oh, how seldom do we feel
　　That pain and tears are best !

We praise Thee for the shining sun,
  For kind and gladsome ways;
When shall we learn, O Lord, to sing
  Through weary nights and days?

Are there no hours of conflict fierce,
  No weary toils and pains,
No watchings, and no bitterness,
  That bring their blessed gains?

That bring their blessed gains full well,
  In truer faith and love,
And patience sweet, and gentleness,
  From our dear Home above?

Teach Thou our weak and wandering hearts
  Aright to read Thy way, —
That Thou, with loving hand dost trace
  Our history every day:

Then Sorrow's face shall be unveiled,
  And we at last shall see
Her eyes are eyes of tenderness,
  Her speech but echoes Thee.

JOHN PAGE HOPPS.

THE HAND OF GOD.

IT is Thy hand, my God !
  My sorrow comes from Thee :
I bow beneath Thy chastening rod ;
  'Tis Love that bruises me.

I would not murmur, Lord,
  Before Thee I am dumb :
Lest I should breathe one murmuring word,
  To Thee for help I come.

My God ! Thy name is Love,
  A Father's hand is Thine ;
With tearful eye I look above,
  And cry, " Thy will be mine."

I know Thy will is right,
  Though it may seem severe ;
Thy path is still unsullied light,
  Though dark it oft appear.

Here my poor heart can rest, —
  My God ! it cleaves to Thee ;
Thy will is Love, Thine end is blest,
  All work for good to me.

JAMES GEORGE DECK. 1843.

GOD KNOWS THE BEST.

GOD knows the best!
 His love can make life's darkness clear,
Chase the heart's winter from the breast,
 And send a summer all the year.
The souls who yield to Him are blest
 With foretastes of their heavenly cheer;
And earthly strife or earthly rest
 It matters not when Home is near.

 God knows the way!
 Trust Him to lead thy steps aright.
Oh, let the path be what it may,
 'Tis smooth to faith, though rough to sight!
Seek not earth's sunshine, nor delay
 By pastures green and waters bright;
For earthly night or earthly day
 It matters little in His light.

 God knows the end!
 His is the Land of love divine:
Thither thy journey all shall tend
 Through storms that beat, or suns that shine.
He shall from every ill defend,
 Though all against thy soul combine;
And earthly foe or earthly friend
 It matters not, if He is thine!

A. G. K.

DE PROFUNDIS.

FOR us — whatever's undergone,
　　Thou knowest, willest what is done.
Grief may be joy misunderstood :
Only the Good discerns the good ;
I trust Thee while my days go on.

I praise Thee while my days go on ;
I love Thee while my days go on !
Through dark and dearth, through fire and frost,
With emptied arms and treasure lost,
I thank Thee while my days go on !

E. B. BROWNING.

HE SENDS IT.

" The very hairs of your head are all numbered."

IS thy path lonely ?　Fear it not, for He
　　Who marks the sparrow's fall is guarding thee ;
And not a star shines o'er thy head by night
But He doth know that it will meet thy sight ;
And not a joy can beautify thy lot,
But tells thee still that thou art unforgot.
Nay, not a grief can darken or surprise,
Dwell in thy heart, or dim with tears thine eyes,
But it is sent in mercy and in love,
To bid thy helplessness seek strength above.

ANONYMOUS.

"BLESSED ARE THEY THAT MOURN."

OH! deem not they are blest alone
  Whose lives a peaceful tenor keep ;
The Power who pities man has shown
  A blessing for the eyes that weep.

The light of smiles shall fill again
  The lids that overflow with tears ;
And weary hours of woe and pain
  Are promises of happier years.

There is a day of sunny rest
  For every dark and troubled night ;
And grief may bide an evening guest,
  But joy shall come with early light.

WILLIAM C. BRYANT.

RICH IN THE LORD.

GOD draws a cloud over each gleaming morn,—
    Would you ask why?
It is because all noblest things are born
    In agony.

Only upon some cross of pain and woe
    God's son may lie:
Each soul, redeemed from self and sin, must know
    Its Calvary.

Yet we should crave neither for joy nor grief ;
  God chooses best :
He only knows our sick soul's best relief,
  And gives us rest.

More than our feeble hearts can ever pine
  For holiness,
That Father, in His tenderness divine,
  Yearneth to bless.

He never sends a joy not meant in love,
  Still less a pain.
Our gratitude the sunlight falls to prove ;
  Our faith, the rain.

In His hands we are safe. We falter on
  Through storm and mire :
Above, beside, around us, there is One
  Will never tire.

What though we fall, and bruised and wounded lie,
  Our lips in dust ?
God's arm shall lift us up to victory :
  In Him we trust.

For neither life nor death, nor things below
  Nor things above,
Shall ever sever us, that we should go
  From His great love.

Frances Power Cobbe. 1859.

THE ANGEL OF PATIENCE.

TO weary hearts, to mourning homes,
God's meekest Angel gently comes :
No power has he to banish pain,
Or give us back our lost again ;
And yet in tenderest love our dear
And Heavenly Father sends him here.

There's quiet in that Angel's glance ;
There's rest in his still countenance !
He mocks no grief with idle cheer,
Nor wounds with words the mourner's ear ;
But ills and woes he may not cure
He kindly trains us to endure.

Angel of Patience ! sent to calm
Our feverish brows with cooling palm ;
To lay the storms of hope and fear,
And reconcile life's smile and tear ;
The throbs of wounded pride to still,
And make our own our Father's will !

O thou who mournest on thy way,
With longings for the close of day !
He walks with thee, that Angel kind,
And gently whispers, " Be resigned ;
Bear up, bear on, the end shall tell
The dear Lord ordereth all things well ! "

A free paraphrase of the German, by JOHN G. WHITTIER.

"YET A LITTLE WHILE."

OH ! for the peace which floweth as a river,
    Making life's desert places bloom and smile.
Oh ! for a faith to grasp heaven's bright forever,
    Amid the shadows of earth's " little while."

A little while for patient vigil-keeping,
    To face the storm, to wrestle with the strong ;
A little while to sow the seed with weeping,
    Then bind the sheaves, and sing the harvest-song.

A little while the earthen pitcher taking
    To wayside brooks from far-off fountains fed ;
Then the parched lip its thirst for ever slaking
    Beside the fulness of the fountain-head.

A little while to keep the oil from failing ;
    A little while Faith's flickering lamp to trim ;
And then, the Bridegroom's coming footstep hailing,
    To haste to meet Him with the bridal hymn.

And He who is at once both gift and Giver,
    The future glory, and the present smile,
With the bright promise of the glad forever,
    Will light the shadows of the little while.

JANE CREWDSON.

PATIENT FAITH.

I HAVE had my happy days,
Followed life through pleasant ways,
  Joys unnumbered bloomed in all :
Now with patient faith I go
Through the desert walks of woe :
  In each life some tears must fall !

Unto Thee I give my heart ;
Life and love may all depart :
  Lord, I love Thee more than life !
Earthly refuge turns to dust ;
Thou my refuge art, my Trust :
  I shall conquer in the strife !

Death may come, but death shall be
Messenger of life to me :
  Can I grieve to see him near ?
In the dark and shadowy vale
Thou, my Father, wilt not fail ;
  And with Thee I feel no fear.

I will take, in patient faith,
Sorrow, darkness, pain, and death,
  Looking only unto Thee :
Lord, I yield me to Thy will !
Be it blessing, be it ill,
  All shall work for good to me.

C. F. Gellert.

THOU VERY PRESENT AID.

THOU very present Aid
　　In suffering and distress,
The soul which still on Thee is stayed
　　Is kept in perfect peace.
　　The soul by faith reclined
　　On his Redeemer's breast
Midst raging storms exults to find
　　An everlasting rest.

　　Sorrow and fear are gone,
　　Whene'er Thy face appears ;
It stills the sighing orphan's moan,
　　And dries the widow's tears.
　　It hallows every cross ;
　　It sweetly comforts me ;
And makes me now forget my loss,
　　And lose myself in Thee.

　　Peace to the troubled heart,
　　Health to the sin-sick mind,
The wounded spirit's Balm Thou art,
　　The Healer of mankind.
　　In deep affliction blest
　　With Thee I mount above,
And sing, triumphantly distrest,
　　Thine all-sufficient Love.

CHARLES WESLEY. 1749

TRUST IN SORROW.

OH let him, whose sorrow
   No relief can find,
Trust in God, and borrow
   Ease for heart and mind.

God will never leave thee ;
   All thy wants He knows,
Feels the pains that grieve thee,
   Sees thy cares and woes.

Raise thine eyes to heaven
   When thy spirits quail,
When, by tempests driven,
   Heart and courage fail.

When in grief we languish,
   He will dry the tear,
Who His children's anguish
   Soothes with succor near.

HYMNS ANCIENT AND MODERN.

LYING STILL.

O LORD my God, do Thou Thy holy will.
   I will lie still :
I will not stir, lest I forsake Thine arm,
   And break the charm
Which lulls me, clinging to my Father's breast
   In perfect rest.

J. KEBLE.

PATIENCE.

FOR patience, when the rough winds blow!
    For patience, when our hopes are fading, —
When visible things all backward go,
    And nowhere seems the power of aiding!
God still enfolds thee with his viewless hand,
And leads thee surely to the Fatherland.

For patience! after bitter ways
    Thy forward path will bloom with blessing.
Faith boldly sets its foot and gaze,
    O'er heights and depths its errands pressing.
Thro' vales of humblest thought it journeys down;
Hence trusts in God to mount and reach its crown.

For patience, heart, till He shall call,
    His " Enter ye," benignly saying;
And though the world shall break and fall,
    Hold on, confiding, watching, praying;
For soon it ends, all need of patience o'er;
Each step still nearer to the Father's door.

N. L. FROTHINGHAM.
Tr. from the German.

TRANSVERSE AND PARALLEL.

MY will, dear Lord, from Thine doth run
    Too oft a different way;
'Tis hard to say, " Thy will be done, "
    In every darkened day!

My heart grows chill
To see Thy will
Turn all life's gold to gray.

My will is set to gather flowers,
  Thine blights them in my hand ;
Mine reaches for life's sunny hours,
  Thine leads through shadow-land ;
        And all my days
        Go on in ways
I cannot understand.

Yet more and more this truth doth shine
  From failure and from loss,
The will that runs transverse to Thine
  Doth thereby make its cross:
        Thine upright will
        Cuts straight and still
Through pride and dream and dross.

But if in parallel to Thine
  My will doth meekly run,
All things in heaven and earth are mine,
  My will is crossed by none ;
        Thou art in me,
        And I in Thee. —
Thy will — and mine — are done !

W. M. L. Jay.

THE ETERNAL YEARS.

HOW shalt thou bear the Cross that now
So dread a weight appears ?
Keep quietly to God, and think
Upon the Eternal Years.

Thy self-upbraiding is a snare,
Though meekness it appears ;
More humbling is it far for thee
To face the Eternal Years.

Brave quiet is the thing for thee,
Chiding thy scrupulous fears ;
Learn to be real from the thought
Of the Eternal Years.

Bear gently, suffer like a child,
Nor be ashamed of tears ;
Kiss the sweet Cross, and in thy heart
Sing of the Eternal Years.

He practises all virtue well,
Who his own Cross reveres,
And lives in the familiar thought
Of these Eternal Years.

F. W. FABER.

THE COMPLAINT OF A PILGRIM.

" O LORD, my God, the way is rough and long ;
  And I through weariness am faint and failing."
" I am thy Staff, and I will strengthen thee,
  Though earthly help is vain and unavailing."

" There is no water in this weary land,
  While thirst consumes my parched and fainting soul."
" Come unto Me ! of living streams the Fount ;
  I will refresh thee ; I will make thee whole.

" Fold not the darkness fondly round thy heart,
  Think of My mercy sweet, and comfort thee,
My poor, unworthy Child ; for Mine thou art,
  And sin alone can snatch My Child from Me.

" I leave thee never ; thou art not alone,
  And with thine own and thee Mine angels dwell :
Possess thy soul in patience ; freely give
  Me love for Love, and all shall yet be well.

" The time is short. They that now weep, ere long
  Shall be as though they wept not ; they that mourn
Be comforted, for I will comfort them ,
  And sweet shall be their glad thanksgiving song."

ELIA. From " Lyra Mystica."

SONG OF RESIGNATION.

THOU sweet, beloved Will of God,
  My anchor-ground, my fortress-hill,
The spirit's silent fair abode,
  In thee I hide me and am still.

O Will, that willest good alone,
  Lead thou the way, thou guidest best ;
A silent child, I follow on,
  And trusting lean upon thy breast.

God's will doth make the bitter sweet,
  And all is good when it is done ;
Unless God's will doth hallow it,
  The glory of all joy is gone.

And if in gloom I see thee not,
  I lean upon thy love unknown ;
In me thy blessed will is wrought,
  If I will nothing of my own.

O Will, in me thy work be done,
  For time and for eternity ;
Give joy or sorrow, — all is one
  To the blest soul that loveth thee.

GERHARD TERSTEEGEN.

ART THOU WEARY?

ART thou weary, art thou languid,
     Art thou sore distrest?
"Come to me," saith One, "and coming
     Be at rest."

Hath he marks to lead me to him,
     If he be my guide?
" In his feet and hands are wound-prints ;
     And his side. "

Is there diadem, as monarch,
     That his brow adorns?
" Yea, a crown, in very surety,
     But of thorns."

If I find him, if I follow,
     What his guerdon here?
" Many a sorrow, many a labor,
     Many a tear."

If I still hold closely to him,
     What hath he at last?
" Sorrow vanquished, labor ended,
     Jordan passed ! "

If I ask him to receive me,
    Will he say me nay?
"Not till earth, and not till heaven,
    Pass away!"

Finding, following, keeping, struggling,
    Is he sure to bless?
"Angels, martyrs, prophets, virgins,
    Answer, Yes!"

JOHN MASON NEALE.
From the Greek of STEPHEN THE SABAITE.

OUR STRONGHOLD OF HOPE.

GOD liveth ever!
    Wherefore, Soul, despair thou never!
Our God is good, in every place
    His love is known, His help is found,
His mighty arm and tender grace
    Bring good from ills that hem us round;
      Easier than we think can He
      Turn to joy our agony.
      Soul, remember 'mid thy pains,
      God o'er all for ever reigns.

God liveth ever !
Wherefore, Soul, despair thou never !
He who can earth and heaven control,
  Who spreads the clouds o'er sea and land,
Whose presence fills the mighty Whole,
  In each true heart is close at hand ;
      Love Him, He will surely send
      Help and joy that never end.
      Soul, remember in thy pains,
      God o'er all for ever reigns.

God liveth ever !
Wherefore, Soul, despair thou never !
When sins and follies long forgot
  Upon thy tortured conscience prey ;
Oh, come to God, and fear Him not,
  His love shall sweep them all away ;
      Pains of hell at look of His
      Change to calm content and bliss.
      Soul, remember in thy pains
      God o'er all for ever reigns.

God liveth ever !
Wherefore, Soul, despair thou never !
Those whom the thoughtless world forsakes,
  Who stand bewildered with their woe,
God gently to His bosom takes,
  And bids them all His fulness know.

In thy sorrows' swelling flood,
Own His hand who seeks thy good.
Soul, forget not in thy pains
God o'er all for ever reigns.

God liveth ever !
Wherefore, Soul, despair thou never !
What though thou tread with bleeding feet
  A thorny path of grief and gloom ?
Thy God will choose the way most meet
  To lead thee heavenwards, lead thee home.
    For this life's long night of sadness
    He will give thee peace and gladness.
    Soul, remember in thy pains
    God o'er all for ever reigns.

J. F. ZIHN. 1682.

TRIALS.

TRIALS must and will befall ;
    But with humble faith to see
Love inscribed upon them all, —
    This is happiness to me.

Trials make the promise sweet ;
    Trials give new life to prayer ;
Trials bring me to His feet,
    Lay me low, and keep me there.

WILLIAM COWPER.

WALDENSIAN HYMN.

WHEN clouds are hovering o'er us,
　　And tempests chafe the sea ;
When death frowns dark before us,
　Where shall Thy people flee ?
　　　Where shall the heart
　　　Its fears impart ?
　To Thee, our God, to Thee !

Safe, safe amidst the hurricane
　Thy servants shall not fear ;
The rending sky, the roaring main
　Are music to the ear :
　　　For He who binds
　　　The waves and winds,
　Our God, is ever near.

Our frail bark shall not founder ;
　Subdued at Thy behest,
The storm that howls around her
　Thy look can lull to rest ;
　　　Our faith in Thee
　　　The helm shall be, —
　The sunshine of the breast.

WILLIAM BEATTIE.   1866.

LOVE OF THE CROSS.

O FATHER ! let me bear the cross ;
　　Make it my daily food ;
Though with it Thou dost send the loss
　　Of every other good.

Take house and lands and earthly fame, —
　　To all I am resigned ;
But let me make one earnest claim :
　　Leave, leave the Cross behind !

I know it costs me many tears,
　　But they are tears of bliss ;
And moments there outweigh the years
　　Of selfish happiness.

The Cross is Love, to action given,
　　Love "seeking not its own ;"
But finding truth and peace and heaven
　　In good to others shown.

The Cross doth live in God's great life,
　　In Christ's dear heart doth shine ;
And how, without its pains and strife,
　　Shall God and Christ be mine ?

THOMAS C. UPHAM.

WHAT MY FRIEND SAID TO ME.

TROUBLE? dear friend, I know her not.　God sent
　　His angel Sorrow on my heart to lay
Her hand in benediction, and to say,
" Restore, O child, that which thy Father lent,
For He doth now recall it," long ago.
　His blessed angel Sorrow !　She has walked
　For years beside me, and we two have talked
As chosen friends together.　Thus I know
Trouble and Sorrow are not near of kin.
　Trouble distrusteth God, and ever wears
　Upon her brow the seal of many cares ;
But Sorrow oft has deepest peace within.
　She sits with Patience in perpetual calm,
Waiting till Heaven shall send the healing balm.

DUBLIN UNIVERSITY MAGAZINE.

FOREBODING.

WHAT weight is this which presses on my soul ?
　　Powerless to rise, I sink amidst the dust :
The days in solemn cycle o'er me roll,
　While, praying, I can only wait and trust.

Trust the dear Hand that all my life has led
　Through pastures green, by waters pure and still ;
If now He leads me through dark ways and dread,
　Shall I dare murmur, whatsoe'er His will ?

LIPPINCOTT'S MAGAZINE.

THE CHASTENING OF THE LORD.

O SPECK in creation!
　　How canst thou complain,
Though sore thy probation
　　Of sorrow and pain?
Forgetting that life
　　Is no season of ease,
But of watching and strife,
　　Till the battle shall cease.

Those whom I hold dearest
　　I chasten and prove
By trials severest, —
　　The sign of my love:
By the sharpness of pain
　　Their faith is made sure,
Till the joys they attain
　　That for ever endure.

For nought canst thou tender
　　More dear to thy Lord
Than thus to surrender
　　Thyself to His word;
With never a moan
　　All thy sufferings bear;
Bring those to His throne.
　　As thine offering there.

FROM AN ANCIENT LATIN POEM
Tr. by J. GREGORY SMITH.

THY WILL BE DONE.

MY God and Father, while I stray,
Far from my home, in life's rough way,
Oh! teach me from my heart to say,
"Thy will be done!"

Though dark my path and sad my lot,
Let me "be still," and murmur not;
Or breathe the prayer divinely taught,
"Thy will be done!"

What though in lonely grief I sigh
For friends beloved, no longer nigh,
Submissive still would I reply,
"Thy will be done!"

Though Thou hast called me to resign
What most I prized, it ne'er was mine:
I have but yielded what was Thine:—
"Thy will be done!"

Should grief or sickness waste away
My life in premature decay;
My Father! still I strive to say,
"Thy will be done!"

Let but my fainting heart be blest
With Thy sweet Spirit for its guest;
My God! to Thee I leave the rest:
    "Thy will be done!"

Renew my will from day to day!
Blend it with Thine; and take away
All that now makes it hard to say,
    "Thy will be done!"

CHARLOTTE ELLIOTT. 1836.

SUBMISSION.

GOD'S right-hand angel, bright and calm, —
    Christ's strengthener in the agony, —
Teach *us* the meaning of that psalm
Of fulness only known by thee:
"Thy will be done!" We sit alone,
And grief within our heart grows strong
With passionate moaning, till thou come,
    And turn it to a song.

Come when the days go heavily,
Weighed down with burdens hard to bear;
When joy and hope fail utterly,
And leave us fronted by despair.
Come not with flattering earthly light,
But with those clear grand eyes that see
Beyond the dark, beyond the bright,
    Straight toward Eternity.

Teach us to work when work seems vain,
This is half victory over fate, —
To match ourselves against our pain ;
The rest is done when we can wait.
Unseal our eyes to see how rife
With bloom this thorny path may be ;
And how it leads to heights of life
    Which only thou canst see.

Content thee (so the angel saith):
Thy minor makes the triumph strain
Sound sweeter on celestial breath,
And God has use for all thy pain.
His joy thy struggling soul may reach ;
From the strong slain comes sweetness still :
And God lets suffering only teach
    Some best revealings of His will.

Then strike within our hearts the key !
Though only sorrow's note it give,
Yet fit us for Thy harmony,
And teach us how to live !
O patient Watcher over all !
If broken lives may best complete
Thy circle, let our fragments fall
    An offering at Thy feet.

CARL SPENCER.

PER PACEM AD LUCEM.

I DO not ask, O Lord, that life may be
      A pleasant road ;
I do not ask that Thou wouldst take from me
      Aught of its load ;

For one thing only, Lord, dear Lord, I plead,
      Lead me aright —
Though strength should falter, and though heart should
      bleed —
      Through Peace to Light.

I do not ask my cross to understand,
      My way to see ;
Better in darkness just to feel Thy hand,
      And follow Thee.

Joy is like restless day ; but peace divine
      Like quiet night ;
Lead me, O Lord, — till perfect Day shall shine,
      Through Peace to Light.

ADELAIDE A. PROCTER.

AS THOU WILT.

AS Thou wilt, my God! I ever say;
     What Thou wilt is ever best for me;
What have I to do with earthly care,
     Since to-morrow I may leave with Thee?
Lord, Thou knowest, I am not my own,
All my hope and help depend on Thee alone.

As Thou wilt! still I can believe,
     Never did the word of promise fail;
Faith can hold it fast, and feel it sure,
     Though temptations cloud and fears assail.
Why art thou disquieted, my soul,
When thy Father knows and rules the whole?

As Thou wilt! still I can endure; —
     Patiently my daily cross can bear;
Why should I complain, a pardoned child,
     If the children's portion here I share?
As Thou wilt, my Father and my God!
I can drink the cup, and kiss the rod.

As Thou wilt! still I can hope on, —
     Sunshine may return when storms have past;
Thine All-seeing Eye of sleepless love
     Watches o'er my path from first to last.

When Thou wilt, upon the desert plain
Springs may rise anew, and rivers flow again.

As Thou wilt! all life's journey through,
   To Thy will my own I would resign;
If on earth I have but little store,
   Be it so: all heaven shall be mine;
Or if but Thyself, my God, art given,
Nothing more I need, or ask in earth or heaven.

As Thou wilt! when Thine hour has come,
   Let Thy servant, Lord, in peace depart;
Good it is to love and serve Thee here,
   Better to be with Thee where Thou art.
When or where or how the call may be,
It will not come too early or too late for me.

As Thou wilt, O Lord! I ask no more.
   With the promise, Faith pursues her way;
Patience can endure through Sorrow's night;
   Hope can look beyond, to Heaven's own day;
Love can wait and trust and labor still:
Life and death shall be according to Thy will!

Neumister.
"Hymns from the Land of Luther."

THE GUIDING HAND.

IS this the way, my Father? — 'Tis, my child.
Thou must pass through this tangled, dreary wild,
If thou wouldst reach the city undefiled,
  Thy peaceful home above.

But enemies are round. — Yes, child, I know
That where thou least expectest thou'lt find a foe ;
But victor thou shalt prove o'er all below,
  Only seek strength above.

My Father, it is dark. — Child, take my hand,
Cling close to me ; I'll lead thee through the land ;
Trust my all-seeing care, so shalt thou stand
  'Midst glory bright above.

My footsteps seem to slide. — Child, only raise
Thine eye to me ; then in these slippery ways
I will hold up thy goings ; thou shalt praise
  Me for each step above.

O Father, I am weary. — Lean thy head
Upon my breast. It was my love that spread
Thy rugged path ; hope on, till I have said :
  " Now come and rest above."

ANONYMOUS.

THY WILL BE DONE.

WE see not, know not; all our way
Is night, — with Thee alone is day :
From out the torrent's troubled drift,
Above the storm our prayers we lift,
Thy will be done !

The flesh may fail, the heart may faint,
But who are we to make complaint,
Or dare to plead, in times like these,
The weakness of our love of ease ?
Thy will be done !

We take with solemn thankfulness
Our burden up, nor ask it less,
And count it joy that even we
May suffer, serve, or wait for Thee,
Whose will be done !

Strike, Thou the Master, we Thy keys,
The anthem of the destinies !
The minor of Thy loftier strain,
Our hearts shall breathe the old refrain,
Thy will be done !

JOHN G. WHITTIER.

'TIS ALL THE SAME TO ME.

'TIS all the same to me, —
    Sorrow, and strife, and pining want, and pain!
Whate'er it is, it cometh all from Thee,
    And 'tis not mine to doubt Thee or complain.

Thou knowest what is best;
    And who but Thee, O God, hath power to know?
In Thy great will my trusting heart shall rest;
    Beneath that will my humble head shall bow.

Then what Thou pleasest send:
    To order all my destiny is Thine.
With Thee, in all Thy purposes, to blend
    In unity of heart, let that be mine.

No questions will I ask.
    Do what Thou wilt, my Father and my God:
Obedience is my consecrated task,
    Though Thou shouldst lead me where Thy martyrs
        trod.

Alike, all pleases well.
    Since living faith hath made it understood, —
Within the shadowy folds of sorrow dwell
    The seeds of life and everlasting good.

THOMAS C. UPHAM.

REMEMBER ME.

" Remember me, O my God, for good." — NEH. xiii. 31.

MY God, forget me not
   In sorrow's evil day,
When dark the shadows fall
   Around my pilgrim way.
To Thy sure word of hope
   Let me for refuge flee ;
In mercy, then, for good,
   O Lord, remember me !

My God, forget me not,
   When low before Thy throne
I seek to spread my cares,
   And make my wishes known.
A Father's gracious face,
   By faith, then let me see ;
I am Thy loving child, —
   O Lord, remember me !

My God, forget me not,
   When my poor soul is dumb,
And only sighs and tears,
   Instead of words, will come.
Though even sighs should cease,
   Desires are known to Thee ; —
In pity, then, and love,
   O Lord, remember me !

My God, forget me not,
  When all around is bright ;
Undazzled let me walk
  Amid the sunshine light.
Give me a quiet mind,
  From earthly bondage free ;
Be Thou my chiefest joy, —
  O Lord, remember me !

My God, forget me not,
  When this forgetful heart
Is tempted from Thy ways
  To wander and depart.
Give me to find no rest
  Till I return to Thee,
In lowly penitence, —
  O Lord, remember me !

My God, forget me not,
  When my last hour is near,
And all the things of earth
  Grow dim or disappear.
Through the dark valley's shade
  Thy glory let me see ;
My light in life, in death, —
  O Lord, remember me !

W. von Bianowsky.
From " Hymns from the Land of Luther.'

BE STILL!

PEACE! Be still!
In this night of sorrow bow,
O my heart! contend not thou!
What befalls thee is God's will —
Peace! Be still!

Peace! Be still!
All thy murmuring words are vain, —
God will make the riddle plain:
Wait His word and bear His will. —
Peace! Be still!

Hold thee still!
Though the good Physician's knife
Seem to touch thy very life,
Death alone he means to kill. —
Hold thee still!

Shepherd mine!
From thy fulness give me still
Faith to do and bear Thy will,
Till the morning light shall shine,
Shepherd mine!

FROM THE GERMAN

SONNET.

COUNT each affliction, whether light or grave,
  God's messenger sent down to thee.   Do thou
With courtesy receive him : rise and bow ;
And, ere his shadow pass thy threshold, crave
Permission first his heavenly feet to lave,
Then lay before him all thou hast.   Allow
No cloud of passion to usurp thy brow,
Or mar thy hospitality, no wave
Of mortal tumult to obliterate
Thy soul's marmoreal calmness.   Grief should be
Like joy, majestic, equable, sedate,
Confirming, cleansing, raising, making free,
Strong to consume small troubles ; to commend
Great thoughts, grave thoughts, thoughts lasting to the
      end.   AUBREY DE VERE.

THE WILL OF GOD.

WHEN obstacles and trials seem
      Like prison-walls to be,
I do the little I can do,
    And leave the rest to Thee.

Ill that He blesses is our good,
    And unblest good is ill ;
And all is right that seems most wrong,
    If it be His sweet Will !

                      F. W. FABER.

SOVEREIGN RULER OF THE SKIES.

SOVEREIGN Ruler of the skies,
  Ever gracious, ever wise,
All my times are in Thy hand,
All events at Thy command.

Times of sickness, times of health,
Times of penury and wealth;
Times of trial and of grief,
Times of triumph and relief.

O Thou Gracious, Wise, and Just!
In Thy hands my life I trust:
Have I something dearer still?
I resign it to Thy will.

Thee at all times will I bless;
Having Thee, I all possess;
How can I bereavèd be,
Since I cannot part with Thee?

JOHN RYLAND. 1777.

"THE E'EN BRINGS A' HAME."

UPON the hills the wind is sharp and cold,
  The sweet young grasses wither on the wold,
And we, O Lord, have wandered from Thy fold;
  But evening brings us home.

Among the mists we stumbled, and the rocks
Where the brown lichen whitens, and the fox
Watches the straggler from the scattered flocks ;
    But evening brings us home.

The sharp thorns prick us, and our tender feet
Are cut and bleeding, and the lambs repeat
Their pitiful complaints, — oh, rest is sweet
    When evening brings us home !

We have been wounded by the hunters' darts ;
Our eyes are very heavy, and our hearts
Search for Thy coming ; when the light departs,
    And evening brings us home.

The darkness gathers. Through the gloom no star
Rises to guide us. We have wandered far, —
Without Thy lamp we know not where we are ;
    At evening, bring us home.

The clouds are round us, and the snow-drifts thicken ;
O Thou, dear Shepherd ! leave us not to sicken
In the waste night, our tardy footsteps quicken ;
    At evening, bring us home.

Fraser's Magazine.

MIDWINTER.

MIDWINTER comes to-morrow,
    My welcome guest to be :
White-haired, wide-winged Sorrow,
    With Christmas gifts for me.
Thy angel, God!— I thank Thee still.
Thy will be done, — Thy better will !

I thank Thee, Lord ! — the whiteness
    Of winter on my heart
Shall keep some glint of brightness,
    Though sun and stars depart.
Thou smilest on the snow : Thy will
Is dread and drear, but lovely still.

W. J. LINTON.

PILGRIM OF EARTH.

PILGRIM of earth, who art journeying to heaven !
    Heir of eternal life ! Child of the day !
Cared for, watched over, beloved, and forgiven —
    Art thou discouraged because of the way?

Weary and thirsty — no water-brook near thee,
    Press on, nor faint at the length of the way ;
The God of thy life will assuredly hear thee, —
    He will provide thee with strength for the day.

Break through the brambles and briers that obstruct thee,
   Dread not the gloom and the blackness of night ;
Lean on the Hand that will safely conduct thee,
   Trust to His eye to whom darkness is light.

Be trustful, be steadfast, whatever betide thee ;
   Only one thing do thou ask of the Lord, —
Grace to go forward wherever He guide thee,
   Simply believing the truth of His word.

ANONYMOUS.

WHEREFORE ?

O THOU ! whose gently chastening hand
   In mercy deals the blow,
Make but Thy servant understand
   Wherefore Thou lay'st me low !

I ask Thee not the rod to spare,
   While thus Thy love I see ;
But, oh, let every suffering bear
   Some message, Lord, from Thee !

Oh, silence Thou this murmuring will,
   Nor bid Thy rough wind stay,
Till with a furnace hotter still
   My dross is purged away !

E. M.

Sickness.

HYMN FOR SICKNESS.

GOD! whom I as Love have known,
   Thou hast sickness laid on me,
   And these pains are sent of Thee,
Under which I burn and moan;
All that plagues my body now,
   All that wasteth me away,
   Pressing on me night and day,
Love ordains, for Love art Thou!

Suffering is the work now sent;
   Nothing can I do but lie
   Suffering as the hours go by;
All my powers to this are bent:
Suffering is my gain; I bow
   To my heavenly Father's will,
   And receive it hushed and still;
Suffering is my worship now.

Let my soul beneath her load
   Faint not, through the o'erwearied flesh ;
   Let her hourly drink afresh
Love and peace from Thee, my God.
Let the body's pain and smart
   Hinder not her flight to thee,
   Nor the calm Thou givest me ;
Keep Thou up the sinking heart,

Grant me never to complain,
   Make me to Thy will resigned,
   With a quiet humble mind,
Cheerful on my bed of pain.
Wholly Thine, — my faith is sure,
   Whether life or death be mine,
   I am safe if I am Thine ;
For 'tis Love that makes me pure.

RICHTER. 1713.

FOR ONE VISITED WITH SICKNESS.

O THOU ! whose wise, paternal Love
   Hath brought my active vigor down,
Thy will I thankfully approve ;
   And, prostrate at Thy gracious throne,
I offer up my life's remains,
I choose the state my God ordains.

Cast as a broken vessel by,
  Thy work I can no longer *do ;*
Yet while a daily death I die,
  Thy power I may in weakness show:
My patience may Thy glory raise,
My speechless woe proclaim Thy praise.

But since without Thy Spirit's might
  Thou know'st I nothing can endure,
The help I ask in Jesu's right,
  The strength He did for me procure,
Father, abundantly impart,
And arm with love my feeble heart.

This single good I humbly crave ;
  This single good on me bestow ;
And when my one desire I have,
  Let every other blessing go.
Ah, do not, Lord, my suit deny!
I only want to love, and die.

Or let me live, of love possessed,
  In weakness, weariness, and pain ;
The anguish of my laboring breast,
  The daily cross I still sustain
For Him that languished on the tree,
But lived, before He died, for me.

Charles Wesley.

HE DOETH ALL THINGS WELL.

I HOPED that with the brave and strong
  My portioned task might lie;
To toil amid the busy throng,
  With purpose pure and high;
But God has fixed another part,
  And He has fixed it well;
I said so with my breaking heart
  When first this anguish fell.

These weary hours will not be lost,
  These days of misery,
These nights of darkness, tempest-tossed,
  Can I but turn to Thee;
With secret labor to sustain
  In patience every blow,
To gather fortitude from pain,
  And holiness from woe.

If Thou shouldst bring me back to life,
  More humble I should be,
More wise, more strengthened for the strife,
  More apt to lean on Thee;
Should death be standing at the gate,
  Thus should I keep my vow;
But, Lord! whatever be my fate,
  Oh, let me serve Thee now!

ANNE BRONTË.

RESIGNATION.

O LORD, my best desire fulfil,
　　And help me to resign
Life, health, and comfort to Thy will,
　　And make Thy pleasure mine.

Why should I shrink from Thy command,
　　Whose love forbids my fears,
Or tremble at the gracious hand
　　That wipes away my tears?

No, rather let me freely yield
　　What most I prize to Thee,
Who never hast a good withheld,
　　Or wilt withhold, from me.

William Cowper. 1779.

ALL, ALL IS KNOWN TO THEE.

*" When my spirit was overwhelmed within me, then Thou knewest
my path."*

MY God, whose gracious pity I may claim,
　　Calling Thee Father, sweet, endearing name!
The sufferings of this weak and weary frame,
　　All, all are known to Thee.

From human eyes 'tis better to conceal
Much that I suffer, much I hourly feel;
But, oh! this thought doth tranquillize and heal, —
    All, all is known to Thee.

Each secret conflict with indwelling sin,
Each sickening fear I ne'er the prize shall win,
Each pang from irritation, turmoil, din, —
    All, all are known to Thee.

When in the morning unrefreshed I wake,
Or in the night but little sleep can take,
This brief appeal submissively I make, —
    All, all is known to Thee.

Nay, all by Thee is ordered, chosen, planned:
Each drop that fills my daily cup; Thy hand
Prescribes for ills none else can understand;
    All, all is known to Thee.

And this continued feebleness, this state
Which seems to unnerve and incapacitate,
Will work the cure my hopes and prayers await,
    That can I leave to Thee.

ADELAIDE L. NEWTON. 1824–1854.

RESTING ON GOD.

WHEN languor and disease invade
   This trembling house of clay,
'Tis sweet to look beyond the cage,
   And long to fly away.

Sweet on His faithfulness to rest,
   Whose love can never end;
Sweet on His covenant of grace
   For all things to depend.

Sweet in the confidence of faith
   To trust His firm decrees;
Sweet to lie passive in His hand,
   And know no will but His.

If such the sweetness of the stream,
   What must the Fountain be,
Where saints and angels draw their bliss
   Immediately from Thee!

              A. M. TOPLADY. 1777.

IN SICKNESS.

NOT more than I have strength to bear,
   Thy mercy, Lord, will lay on me;
   Pain shall not always last;
   Sweet ease is coming fast.
On my sick bed, free from care,
Present Helper! praise I Thee!

When me the world so much distraught,
Thy Hand to solitude did bring;
 And, when the fight I fled,
 To deeper warfare led;
And through pain my heart hath taught
A new and patient song to sing.

And shall I drain this cup of woe?
Ah, Lord! Thou knowest flesh is weak!
 Forgive the tears that start
 From weary eyes and heart!
Now Thy tender pity show,
Give the patient faith I seek.

The pain which racks and weakens me,
Drives far away my sleep's soft rest;
 The long dark nights may hear
 My groans of grief and fear.
How poor I find man's help to be!
But Thou canst still my throbbing breast!

Thy will may choose and give command
How long the trial hour shall last:
 And though on this dark field
 My whole life-strength should yield,
Passing to the better land,
Still my heart shall hold Thee fast!

From the German, tr. by ANNA WARNER

HOPE IS BETTER THAN EASE.

WISH not, dear friends, my pain away:
  Wish me a wise and thankful heart,
With God, in all my griefs, to stay,
  Nor from His loved correction start.

In Life's long sickness evermore
  Our thoughts are tossing to and fro :
We change our posture o'er and o'er,
  But cannot rest, nor cheat our woe.

Were it not better to lie still,
  Let Him strike home, and bless the rod ;
Never so safe as when our will
  Yields undiscerned by all but God ?

Thy precious things, whate'er they be
  That haunt and vex thee, heart and brain,
Look to the cross, and thou shalt see
  How thou mayst turn them all to gain.

JOHN KEBLE.

IT IS GOOD FOR ME.

" Thy people shall be willing in the day of Thy power."

I WISHED a flowery path to tread,
  And thought 'twould safely lead to heaven ;
A lonely room, a suffering bed,
  These for my training place were given.

Long I resisted, mourned, complained, —
  Wished any other lot my own :
Thy purpose, Lord, unchanged remained, —
  What Wisdom planned, Love carried on.

Year after year I turned away,
  But marred was every scheme I planned ;
Still the same lesson, day by day,
  Was placed before me by Thy hand.

At length Thy patient, wondrous love,
  Unchanging, tender, pitying, strong,
Availed that stubborn heart to move,
  Which had rebelled, alas ! so long.

Then I was taught by Thee to say,
  " Do with me what to Thee seems best ;
Give, take, whate'er Thou wilt away,
  Health, comfort, usefulness, or rest ;

" Be my whole life in suffering spent ;
  But let me be in suffering Thine, —
Still, O my Lord, I am content,
  Thou now hast made Thy pleasure mine."

CHARLOTTE ELLIOTT.

THE WAYSIDE WATCHER.

HAVE ye known the shadows darken
On weary nights of pain,
And hours that seem to lengthen
Till the night comes round again?
The folded hands seem idle:
If folded at His word,
'Tis a holy service, trust me,
In obedience to the Lord.

None shall e'er lack a service,
Who only seek His will,
And He doth teach His children
To suffer and be still.
In love's deep fount of treasures
Such precious things are stored,
Laid up for you, O blessed,
That wait upon the Lord!

ANNA SHIPTON.

MY PSALM.

O THOU, most present in our paths
When least Thy steps we see!
Amid these wrecks of earthly hopes
I breathe my prayer to Thee.

What though this house Thy hand has built
Must in these ruins fall!
My soul shall rise, sustained by Thee,
Serene above them all.

And pain, which in the long, long hours,
  Keeps on by night and day,
Through these fast crumbling walls to Thee
  Finds a new opening way ;

For through the rents already made
  I see Thy glorious face,
And songs unheard by mortal ears
  Chant Thy redeeming grace.

Oh ! build anew this mortal frame,
  And make it serve Thee still,
Or make these ministries of pain
  Their blessed end fulfil :

That, held and chastened by Thy hand,
  I yet may come to Thee,
Subdued and ripened for the work
  Of immortality.

For there, upon the immortal shores,
  The throngs in white array
Come from these ministries of pain
  To serve Thee night and day.

Edmund H. Sears

"O LORD, I KNOW THAT IN VERY FAITH-
FULNESS THOU HAST AFFLICTED ME."

FOR what shall I praise Thee, my God and my King?
    For what blessings the tribute of gratitude bring?
Shall I praise Thee for pleasure, for health, and for ease,
For the spring of delight, and the sunshine of peace?

Shall I praise Thee for flowers that bloomed on my
    breast;
For joys in perspective, and pleasures possessed?
For the spirits that heightened my day of delight,
And the slumbers that sat on my pillow by night?

For this should I praise Thee; but, if only for this,
I should leave half untold the donation of bliss:
I thank Thee for sickness, for sorrow, for care,
For the thorns I have gathered, the anguish I bear, —

For nights of anxiety, watching, and tears,
A present of pain, a perspective of fears.
I praise Thee, I bless Thee, my King and my God,
For the good and the evil Thy hand hath bestowed.

CAROLINE WILSON

Sickness.

EVENING PRAYER IN SICKNESS.

LORD, a whole long day of pain
    Now at last is o'er!
Ah, how much we can sustain
    I have felt once more;
Felt how frail are all our powers,
    And how weak our trust;
If Thou help not, these dark hours
    Crush us to the dust.

Draw my weary heart away
    From this gloom and strife,
And these fever-pains allay
    With the dew of life;
Thou canst calm the troubled mind;
    Thou its dread canst still;
Teach me to be all resigned
    To my Father's will.

Then, if I must wake and weep
    All the long night through,
Thou the watch with me wilt keep,
    Friend and Guardian true;
In the darkness Thou wilt speak
    Lovingly with me,
Though my heart may vainly seek
    Words to breathe to Thee.

Wheresoe'er my couch is made,
  In Thy hands I lie,
And to Thee alone for aid
  Turns my restless eye ;
Let my prayer grow weary never,
  Strengthen Thou the oppressed ;
In Thy shadow, Lord, for ever,
  Let me gently rest.

HEINRICH PUCHTA.

FOR A WAKEFUL NIGHT.

NOW darkness over all is spread,
  No sounds the stillness break ;
Ah ! when shall these sad hours be fled,
  Am I alone awake ?

Ah no ! I do not wake alone,
  Alone I do not sleep :
Around me ever watcheth One
  Who wakes with those who weep.

On earth it is so dark and drear,
  With Him so calm and bright,
The stars in solemn radiance clear
  Shine there through all our night.

'Tis when the lights of earth are gone,
　The heavenly glories shine ;
When other comfort I have none,
　Thy comfort, Lord, is mine.

Be still, my throbbing heart, be still,
　Cast off thy weary load,
And make His holy will thy will,
　And rest upon thy God.

How many a time the night hath come !
　Yet still returned the day ;
How many a time thy cross, thy gloom,
　Ere now hath passed away !

And these dark hours of anxious pain
　That now oppress thee sore,
I know will vanish soon again,
　Then I shall fear no more :

For when the night hath lasted long,
　We know the morn is near ;
And when the trial's sharp and strong,
　Our Help shall soon appear.

PASTOR JOSEPHSEN.

THOU WILT NOT FORSAKE ME.

AND wilt Thou now forsake me, Lord?
    I feel it cannot be;
No earthly tongue can ever tell
    What Thou hast been to me.

Through all the changing scenes of life
    Thy love hath sheltered me;
And wilt Thou now forget Thy child?
    I feel it cannot be.

Thy love hath been my heritage
    Through many a weary year;
I've trusted to Thy promises,
    And Thou hast dried each tear.

And now when youth and health and strength
    And energy have fled,
The shades of evening peacefully
    Shall close around my head.

And when in all the helplessness
    Of death I turn to Thee,
Thou wilt not then forsake me, Lord:
    I feel it cannot be.

ANONYMOUS.

THE RESIGNATION.

LONG have I viewed, long have I thought,
  And held with trembling hand this bitter draught :
'Twas just now to my lips applied ;
Nature shrank in, and all my courage died, —
  But now resolved and firm I'll be,
Since, Lord, 'tis mingled and reached out by Thee.

  Take all, great God : I will not grieve ;
But still will wish that I had still to give.
  I hear Thy voice ; Thou biddest me quit
My paradise, — I bless and do submit.
  I will not murmur at Thy word,
Nor beg Thy angel to sheathe up his sword.

JOHN NORRIS. 1657-1711.

"BE NOT THOU FAR FROM ME, O LORD; O MY STRENGTH, HASTE THEE TO HELP ME."

PSALM XXII. 19.

FORSAKE me not, my God : my heart is sinking,
    Bowed down with faithless fears, and bodings vain ;
Busied with dark imaginings, and drinking
  Th' anticipated cup of grief and pain ;
But, Lord, I lean on Thee, Thy staff and rod
    Shall guide my lot ;
I will not fear, if Thou, my God, my God,
    Forsake me not !

CHARLOTTE ELLIOTT.

I HOLD STILL.

PAIN'S furnace-heat within me quivers,
   God's breath upon the flame doth blow,
And all my heart in anguish shivers
   And trembles at the fiery glow;
And yet I whisper, — As God will!
   And, in His hottest fire, hold still.

He comes and lays my heart, all heated,
   On the hard anvil, minded so
Into His own fair shape to beat it,
   With His great hammer, blow on blow;
And yet I whisper, — As God will!
   And, at His heaviest blows, hold still.

He takes my softened heart, and beats it.
   The sparks fly off at every blow;
He turns it o'er and o'er, and heats it,
   And lets it cool, and makes it glow;
And yet I whisper, — As God will!
   And, in His mighty hand, hold still.

Why should I murmur? for the sorrow
   Thus only longer-lived would be;
Its end may come, and will to-morrow,
   When God has done His work in me;
So I say trusting, — As God will!
   And, trusting to the end, hold still.

He kindles for my profit, purely,
   Affliction's glowing, fiery brand ;
And all His heaviest blows are, surely,
   Inflicted by a Master-hand ;
So I say, praying, — As God will !
   And hope in Him, and suffer still.

JULIUS STURM.
Tr. by CHARLES T. BROOKS

HERE AM I.

MY will would like a life of ease, —
   And power to do, and time to rest, —
And health and strength my will would please,
   But, Lord, I know Thy will is best.

If I have strength to do Thy will,
   That should be power enough for me ;
Whether to work or to sit still
   The appointment of the day may be.

And if by sickness I may grow
   More patient, holy, and resigned ;
Strong health I need not wish to know,
   And greater ease I cannot find.

Lord, I have given my life to Thee,
   And every day and hour is Thine, —
What Thou appointest let them be :
   Thy will is better, Lord, than mine.

ANNA WARNER.

FEEBLE, HELPLESS.

FEEBLE, helpless, how shall I
    Learn to live and learn to die ?
Who, O God, my guide shall be ?
Who shall lead Thy child to Thee ?

Blessèd Father, gracious One,
Thou hast sent Thy holy Son ;
He will give the light I need,
He my trembling steps will lead.

Through this world, uncertain, dim,
Let me ever learn of him ;
From his precepts wisdom draw,
Make his life my solemn law.

Thus in deed, and thought, and word,
Led by Jesus Christ the Lord,
In my weakness thus shall I
Learn to live and learn to die ; —

Learn to live in peace and love,
Like the perfect ones above ; —
Learn to die without a fear,
Feeling Thee, my Father, near.

WILLIAM H. FURNESS.

"IT IS THE LORD: LET HIM DO WHAT SEEMETH HIM GOOD."

I SAMUEL III. 18.

THUS saith the Lord : "Thy days of health are over!"
And, like the mist, my vigor fled away;
Till but a feeble shadow was remaining,
A fragile form fast hasting to decay.
The May of life, with all its blooming flowers, —
The joys of life, in colors bright arrayed, —
The hopes of life, in all their airy promise, —
I saw them in the distance slowly fade :
Then sighs of sorrow in my soul would rise,
Then silent tears would overflow my eyes !
But a warm sunbeam from a higher sphere
Stole through the gloom, and dried up every tear.
Is this Thy will, good Lord? — the strife is o'er,
Thy servant weeps no more.

"From the calm port of safety rudely severed,
Through stormy waves thy shattered bark must go,
And dimly see, amid the darkness sinking,
Nothing but heaven above and depths below!" —
Thus said the Lord ; and, through a raging ocean
Of doubts and fears, my spirit toiled in vain :

15

Ah! many a dove went forth, of hope inquiring,
But none with olive leaf returned again!
    Then groans of anguish in my soul would rise,
    Then tears of bitterness o'erflowed my eyes!
But through the gloom the promised light was given,
From the dark waves I *could* look up to heaven:
Is this Thy will, good Lord? — the strife is o'er,
    Thy servant weeps no more.

HEINRICH MÖWES. 1832.
" Hymns from the Land of Luther."

ONE ARMY OF THE LIVING GOD.

COME, let us join our friends above
    That have obtained the prize,
And on the eagle wings of love
    To joy celestial rise.
Let all the saints terrestrial sing
    With those to glory gone ;
For all the servants of our King,
    In earth and heaven, are one.

One family, we dwell in Him,
    One church, above, beneath,
Though now divided by the stream,
    The narrow stream of death.
One army of the living God,
    To His command we bow,
Part of His host hath crossed the flood,
    And part is crossing now.

CHARLES WESLEY. 1759.

"LORD, LIFT THOU UP THE LIGHT OF THY COUNTENANCE UPON ME."

PSALM IV. 6.

AGAIN the orient light is shining;
  Again on Thee, my God, reclining,
Would I pursue my way:
Would follow where Thy voice shall call me;
Would cling to Thee whate'er befall me,
And, oh! let Thy mild look recall me,
  When I would go astray.

And if, dejected, faint, and weary,
My path to-day seem rough and dreary,
  Oh! let Thy pitying love —
That source of sweetest comfort — cheer me;
And tell me Thou art ever near me,
To strengthen, guide, defend, and hear me,
  My all in all to prove.

Should any earthly thing distress me,
Should suffering, cares, or fears depress me,
  When Thou Thy love hast given?
When Thou wilt leave not nor forsake me,
But meet for Thine own presence make me,
And soon wilt come Thyself to take me
  To dwell with Thee in heaven?

CHARLOTTE ELLIOTT

IN THE HOSPITAL.

" S. S., a Massachusetts sergeant, worn out with heavy marches, wounds, and camp disease, died in —— General Hospital, in November, 1863, in 'perfect peace.' Some who witnessed daily his wonderful sweet patience and content, through great languor and weariness, fancied sometimes they 'could already see the brilliant particles of a halo in the air about his head.' "

I LAY me down to sleep,
    With little thought or care
Whether my waking find
    Me here, — or THERE !

A bowing, burdened head,
    That only asks to rest,
Unquestioning, upon
    A loving Breast.

My good right hand forgets
    Its cunning now ;
To march the weary march
    I know not how.

I am not eager, bold,
    Nor strong, — all that is past ;
I am ready NOT TO DO
    At last, — at last !

My half-day's work is done.
 And this is all my part, —
I give a patient God
 My patient heart ;

And grasp His banner still,
 Though all its blue be dim :
These stripes, no less than stars,
 Lead after Him.   ANONYMOUS.

STRENGTH.

TO A FRIEND NEAR DEATH.

"WHEN I am weak, I'm strong,"
 The great Apostle cried.
The strength that did not to the earth belong,
 The might of Heaven supplied.

"When I am weak, I'm strong,"
 Blind Milton caught that strain,
And flung its victory o'er the ills that throng
 Round Age and Want and Pain.

"When I am weak, I'm strong,"
 Each Christian heart repeats ;
These words will tune its feeblest breath to song,
 And fire its languid beats.

O Holy Strength ! whose ground
 Is in the heavenly land ;
And whose supporting help alone is found
 In God's immortal hand.

O Blessed! that appears
    When fleshly aids are spent;
And girds the mind, when most it faints and fears,
    With trust and sweet content.

It bids us cast aside
    All thoughts of lesser powers;
Give up all hope from changing time and tide,
    And all vain will of ours.

We have but to confess
    That there's but one retreat;
And meekly lay each need and each distress
    Down at the sovereign Feet:

Then, then it fills the place
    Of all we hoped to do;
And sunken nature triumphs in the grace
    That bears us up and through.

A better glow than health
    Flushes the cheek and brow;
The heart is stout with store of nameless wealth:
    We can do all things now.

No less sufficience seek;
    All counsel less is wrong;
The whole world's force is poor and mean and weak:
    "When I am weak, I'm strong."

N. L. FROTHINGHAM.

O THOU, WHOSE ALL-ENLIVENING RAY.

O THOU, whose all-enlivening ray
    Can turn my darkness into day,
Disperse, great God, my mental gloom,
And with Thyself my soul illume.
Though gathering sorrows swell my breast,
Speak but the word, and peace and rest
Shall set my troubled spirit free,
In sweet communion, Lord, with Thee.

What though, in this heart-searching hour,
Thou dim'st my intellectual power;
The gracious discipline I own,
And wisdom seek at Thy blest throne.
Let love divine my bosom sway,
And then my darkness will be day;
No doubts, no fears, shall heave my breast,
For God Himself will be my rest.

BISHOP JEBB.

THE BORDER-LANDS.

FATHER, into Thy loving hands
    My feeble spirit I commit,
While wandering in these Border-Lands
    Until Thy voice shall summon it.

Father, I would not dare to choose
   A longer life, an earlier death ;
I know not what my soul might lose
   By shortened or protracted breath.

These Border-Lands are calm and still,
   And solemn are their silent shades ;
And my heart welcomes them, until
   The light of life's long evening fades.

I hear them spoken of with dread,
   As fearful and unquiet places ;
Shades, where the living and the dead
   Look sadly in each others' faces.

But since Thy hand hath led me here,
   And I have seen the Border-Land ;
Seen the dark river flowing near,
   Stood on its brink, as now I stand ;

There has been nothing to alarm
   My trembling soul : how could I fear
While thus encircled with Thine arm?
   I never felt Thee half so near.

What should appall me in a place
   That brings me hourly nearer Thee ?
When I may almost see Thy face, —
   Surely 'tis here my soul would be.

Euphemia Saxby.

TRUST IN THE LORD AT ALL TIMES.

" Deep calleth unto deep at the noise of Thy water-spouts: all Thy waves and Thy billows are gone over me. Yet the Lord will command His loving-kindness in the day-time, and in the night His song shall be with me, and my prayer unto the God of my life." — Ps. xlii. 7, 8.

GO not far from me, O my Strength,
    Whom all my times obey ;
Take from me any thing Thou wilt,
    But go not Thou away, —
And let the storm that does Thy work
    Deal with me as it may.

On Thy compassion I repose,
    In weakness and distress :
I will not ask for greater ease,
    Lest I should love Thee less :
Oh, 'tis a blessed thing for me
    To need Thy tenderness !

Thy love has many a lighted path
    No outward eye can trace ;
And my heart sees Thee in the deep,
    With darkness on its face,
And communes with Thee 'mid the storm
    As in a secret place.

When I am feeble as a child,
    And flesh and heart give way,
Then on Thy everlasting strength
    With passive trust I stay,
And the rough wind becomes a song,
    The darkness shines like day.

No suffering while it lasts is joy,
    How blest soe'er it be, —
Yet may the chastened child be glad
    His Father's face to see ;
And, oh ! it is not hard to bear,
    What must be borne in Thee.

Safe in Thy sanctifying grace,
    Almighty to restore ;
Borne onward — sin and death behind,
    And love and life before, —
Oh, let my soul abound in hope,
    And praise Thee more and more !

Deep unto deep may call ; but I
    With peaceful heart will say, —
Thy loving-kindness hath a charge
    No waves can take away ;
And let the storm that speeds me home
    Deal with me as it may.

ANNA L. WARING.

SWEET PATIENCE, COME.

SWEET Patience, come!
   With long distress my spirit faints,
And my heart breaks with its complaints;
And eager pain, to find relief,
Solicits even change of grief, —
And unbelief disturbs my trust,
And shakes my hopes — as with a gust
Spring blossoms flutter from the stalk,
And withering lie upon the walk : —
   Sweet Patience, come!

   Sweet Patience, come!
Not from a low and earthly source, —
Waiting, till things shall have their course, —
Not as accepting present pain
In hope of some hereafter gain, —
Not in a dull and sullen calm, —
But as a breath of heavenly balm,
Bidding my weary heart submit
To bear whatever God sees fit :
   Sweet Patience, come!

   Sweet Patience, come!
Tell me my Father hath not shed
One grief too many on my head ;
Tell me His love remembers still
His children, suffering at His will.

How excellent a thought to me
His loving-kindness then shall be !
Then in the shadow of His wings
I'll hide me from all troublous things :
    Sweet Patience, come !
HYMNS OF THE CHURCH MILITANT.

THY HAND SHALL LEAD ME.

O LORD, I grasp Thy hand,
    As onward through the night
I journey to the land
  Of everlasting light.
How safe that hand has led
  Through years of mortal ill !
Sorrow and joy alike have fled ;
  But Thou art with me still.

Oh wondrous, wondrous were
  The paths where Thou didst guide !
Rainbows and storms commingled there,
  But Thou wert by my side.
It was the Lord's highway,
  The way of holiness ;
And, whether bright or dark the day,
  It only rose to bless.

Now that the midnight's gloom
  Stealthily creepeth near ;
Sepulchral shadows from the tomb
  With all their solemn fear, —

O Lord, my helper be,
    Though hidden from my sight !
Thy hand upholds as steadfastly
    In darkness as in light.

Then nerve my sinking faith ;
    Oh, take my hand in Thine !
Thy love is stronger far than death ;
    And, Lord, that love is mine.
It is but one black wave,
    And then a crystal sea ;
One dream of darkness in the grave,
    The morn, — Eternity !

Yes, though Love weep its tears,
    And Hope may scarce endure,
Steadily onward move the years, —
    Our endless home is sure.
A home, O Lord, with Thee !
    A home in Thy embrace, —
Where Faith that followed trustingly
    Shall see Thee, face to face.

LIBBICH.

"LOVEST THOU ME."

I DARE not say "I love Thee," Lord,
   Because I know that every day
Some heedless act or thoughtless word,
   Would contradict the thing I say.

And love that is in words expressed
   Too often proves less deep and true
Than that which moves the loving breast
   To do what Thou wouldst have it do.

Ah! I would gladly be like those
   Who dedicate their lives to Thee;
Whose love no dubious token shows
   Of its heartfelt sincerity.

Sweet peace-makers, whose gentle hands
   Can disentangle household love
From envy's irritating bands,
   That gall it like a trammelled dove.

Kind friends who glide about and bear
   Their little flasks of oil and wine,
To solace every cross and care
   With love less human than divine.

Such works, O Lord, Thou dost allow
   As proofs of love within the heart;
But I, a worn-out vessel now,
   Am laid aside, alone, apart.

And yet I dare not say, " I love,"
   Oh, show me then some other way
By which Thy lonely child may prove
   More than her lips would dare to say !

If calm submission, chastened will,
   And cheerfulness the proofs would be
Of love to Him who loves me still,
   O Father, grant them all to me.

EUPHEMIA SAXBY.

RESIGNATION.

WHY should I not meet gladly all my pain, —
   That holy angel sent to me from God !
Why to that God compassionate complain,
   And ask why I the thorny path have trod ?

Like birds that sleep beneath the mother's wing,
   I cling for rest to the Great Father's heart ;
Though sorrow, death, a thousand arrows fling,
   I vanquish, — thou, my faith, unvanquished art.

Soft as a dove, my prayer soars to Thee,
   Soars to my Father's firmament of blue ;
Keen, the abyss of boundless light to see,
   It murmurs in His ear these accents true :

Accept the incense of a soul resigned,
   Thou Soul of souls, to whom its pangs are known ;
To all but love may I in grief be blind,
   As Thou in giving grief Thy love hast shown.

From the Swedish of VITALIS.

GRAND DIEU, POUR TON PLAISIR.

GRAND Dieu, pour ton plaisir
Je suis dans une cage ;
Ecoute mon ramage ;
C'est-là mon seul desir :
J'aime mon esclavage,
Grand Dieu, pour ton plaisir.

Je chante tout le jour,
Seigneur, c'est pour te plaire ;
Mon extrême misère
Augmente mon amour :
N'ayant point d'autre affaire,
Je chante tout le jour.

Tu l'entends, mon Seigneur,
Cet amoureux langage,
Ignoré du faux sage,
Goûté du chaste cœur,
L'amour a son ramage :
Tu l'entends, mon Seigneur.

Je vis en liberté,
Quoique dans l'esclavage :
L'AMOUR PUR met au large
Le cœur, la volonté :
Dans ma petite cage
Je vis en liberté.

Divine volonté,
Que j'adore et que j'aime !
Plus ma peine est extrême,
Plus j'ai de liberté.
Tous biens sont en toi-même,
Divine volonté.

De ton petit oiseau
Reçois, je te conjure,
Le gazouillant murmure,
Plus tendre qu'il n'est beau ;
Et sois la nourriture
De ton petit oiseau.

MADAME GUYON.

A LITTLE BIRD I AM.*

Written during her ten years' imprisonment in the Bastile.

A LITTLE bird I am,
   Shut from the fields of air,
And in my cage I sit and sing
   To Him who placed me there ;
Well pleased a prisoner to be,
   Because, my God, it pleases Thee !

Naught have I else to do,
   I sing the whole day long ;
And He whom most I love to please
   Doth listen to my song ;

* A free translation of the preceding poem.

16

He caught and bound my wandering wing,
But still He bends to hear me sing.

Thou hast an ear to hear,
  A heart to love and bless ;
And, though my notes were e'er so rude,
  Thou wouldst not hear the less ;
Because Thou knowest, as they fall,
That love, sweet love, inspires them all.

My cage confines me round :
  Abroad I cannot fly ;
But, though my wing is closely bound,
  My heart's at liberty ;
My prison walls cannot control
The flight, the freedom of the soul.

Oh, it is good to soar
  These bolts and bars above,
To Him whose purpose I adore,
  Whose providence I love ;
And in Thy mighty will to find
The joy, the freedom, of the mind !

MADAME GUYON
Tr. by Prof. T. C. UPHAM.

THE WANDERER'S HYMN.

O THOU, by long experience tried,
   Near whom no grief can long abide ;
My Lord!　How full of sweet content,
I pass my years of banishment.

All scenes alike engaging prove
To souls impressed with sacred love ,
Where'er they dwell, they dwell in Thee,
In heaven, on earth, or on the sea.

To me remains nor place nor time :
My country is in every clime ;
I can be calm and free from care
On any shore, since God is there.

While place we seek, or place we shun,
The soul finds happiness in none ;
But, with a God to guide our way,
'Tis equal joy to go or stay.

Could I be cast where Thou art not,
That were indeed a dreadful lot ;
But regions none remote I call,
Secure of finding God in all.

MADAME GUYON.　1689.

"I, PAUL, A PRISONER OF THE LORD."

O COMRADE bold of toil and pain !
   Thy trial how severe,
When severed first by prisoner's chain
   From thy loved labor-sphere !

Say, did impatience first impel
   The heaven-sent bond to break ?
Or couldst thou bear its hindrance well,
   Loitering for Jesu's sake ?

Oh might we know ! for sore we feel
   The languor of delay,
When sickness lets our fainter zeal,
   Or foes block up our way.

Lord ! who Thy thousand years dost wait
   To work the thousandth part
Of Thy vast plan, for us create
   With zeal a patient heart.

JOHN HENRY NEWMAN. 1822.

ON LEAVING HOME FOR A MILDER CLIMATE.

" My presence shall go with thee, and I will give thee rest." — Ex.
xxxiii. 14.

THIS gracious promise, Lord, fulfil,
    Now that I leave a home so dear ;
My soul's sweet home is present still,
    If Thou art near.

Beneath Thy wings if I remain,
    My home ! my hiding-place ! my rest !
Sheltered and safe, and free from pain,
    My soul is blest.

Thy presence fills my mind with peace,
    Brightens the thoughts so dark erewhile,
Bids cares and sad forebodings cease,
    Makes all things smile.

This striking of my pilgrim tent
    No longer mournful will appear,
If Thy reviving presence lent,
    The traveller cheer.

The spacious earth is all Thine own ;
    What land soe'er my steps invite,
That land Thine eye will rest upon
    By day, by night.

I ask not health, I ask not ease ;
   I ask in Thee my rest to find ;
To all Thy sovereign will decrees,
      Be mine resigned !

Whether again my home I see,
   Or yield on foreign shores my breath,
Take not Thy presence, Lord, from me,
      In life or death !

In Thee, my hiding-place divine,
   Be rest throughout life's journeyings given :
Then sweeter, holier rest be mine,
      With Thee in heaven !

CHARLOTTE ELLIOTT.

"BEHOLD, O LORD, FOR I AM IN DISTRESS."

LAMENTATIONS I. 20.

LORD, I am very weak, distrest !
   I languish and can take no rest ;
The remedies uncertain prove,
And heavily the moments move ;
I cannot now look up to Thee,
But, oh, look down, look down on me !

CHARLOTTE ELLIOTT.

AT ANCHOR.

OH! strange it seems to lie at anchor here,
  With the broad mainland whence I sailed so nigh.
Ah, me! I cannot check the blinding tear
When out-bound breezes greet my listening ear,
  And wail about my bark with long-drawn sigh.

For well do I remember that glad day
  When from the shore I launched with merry song,
When bird and breeze and billow seemed to say,
In one glad chorus, "Speed thee! speed away!
  And thou the Golden Shore shalt reach ere long."

Yet patience, heart of mine! A loving Hand
  In haven sure thy poor frail craft has moored.
Doubt not His watchful care, nor once demand
A speedier journey to the longed-for strand,
  Whilst thou the One Great Master hast on board.

Dost thou not know 'tis better thus to be
  At anchor on a fog-enveloped isle
Than tossed about with white sail full and free
On the wild billows of an angry sea,
  Thy rudder and thy reckoning lost the while?

These quiet days of waiting rich may be
  With untold blessings, if thou use them well.
Grave was the Master when thy bark was free,
And now He often speaks fond words to thee,—
  Ay! dearer, sweeter words than thou canst tell.

Perchance the Land I seek is not so far
   As youth's high spirit dreamed in days of yore.
'Twas but a fancy that yon hazy bar,
O'er which I marked each eve the first bright star,
   Formed any part of my fair Golden Shore.

It may be close at hand, I cannot tell.
   I only know the Master guideth true ;
And, though at anchor long, I'll not rebel,
But with fresh courage sing the glad *"All's well!"*
   Till in His own good time, my Port I view !

B. E. E.

THOU ART MY HEALTH.

ON Thee, my Health in sickness,
   My feeble soul is stayed ;
Thy strength in human weakness
   Is perfectly displayed :
Thou never wilt forsake me,
   Who on Thy Love depend ;
But to Thy bosom take me
   Till pain with life shall end.

CHARLES WESLEY. 1767

WAITING.

" Ye have need of patience, that, after ye have done the will of God,
ye might receive the promise." — HEB. x. 36.

AND is there nothing to be done,
   While here, on this sick-bed, I lie?
Should I thus weary to be gone,
   Thus think, 'twere better far to die?

Alas! that very thought declares
   How much remains unhallowed still;
The soul, which God for heaven prepares,
   Has lost her own in His blest will.

And if His work of grace in me
   Were now well nigh consummated,
Contented, willing should I be,
   To lie for years on this sick-bed.

For then, my faith would be so strong,
   Would bring my blessèd Lord so near,
That days, weeks, months, would ne'er seem long,
   With such a Friend my couch to cheer.

Full many a sufferer there has seen
   Such proofs of His transcendent worth,
That e'en their bed of pain has been
   To them a little heaven on earth.

Oh ! grant me now that will resigned,
    That patient, weaned, obedient heart ;
That loving, peaceful, heavenly mind,
    Thy Spirit can alone impart.

Let me not languish e'en for home,
    One wish, one only wish, be mine :
Each hour more holy to become,
    More fully and entirely Thine !

CHARLOTTE ELLIOTT.

"LORD, BE THOU MY HELPER!"

PSALM XXX. 10.

WHEN all outward comfort flies,
    And my heart within me dies,
Hear, oh hear, my trembling sighs !
    Help me, O my Father !

When the day brings pain and grief,
Night, nor respite, nor relief,
Whisper — " These dark hours are brief : "
    Help me, O my Father !

When all human help proves vain,
And my agonizing pain
More than nature can sustain,
    Help me, O my Father !

Thou, Thou only canst relieve me !
Till Thine arms of love receive me,
Whisper — " I will never leave Thee ! "
    Help me, O my Father !

CHARLOTTE ELLIOTT.

THE THOUGHT OF GOD.

TO think of Thee is almost prayer,
  And is outspoken praise ;
And pain can even passive thoughts
  To actual worship raise.

O Lord ! I live always in pain,
  My life's sad under-song, —
Pain in itself not hard to bear,
  But hard to bear so long.

Little sometimes weighs more than much,
  When it has no relief ;
A joyless life is worse to bear
  Than one of active grief.

And yet, O Lord ! a suffering life
  One grand ascent may dare ;
Penance, not self-imposed, can make
  The whole of life a prayer.

All murmurs lie inside Thy Will
  Which are to Thee addressed :
To suffer for Thee is our work ;
  To think of Thee, our rest.

F. W. FABER.

WITH GOD.

GOOD Lord, no strength I have, nor need :
    Within Thy light I lie,
And grow like herb in sunny place,
    While outer storms go by.

Thy pleasant rain my soul doth feed, —
    Thy love like summer rain ;
I faint, but, lo ! thy winds of grace
    Revive my soul again.

I fain would give some perfume out,
    Some bruisèd scent of myrrh ;
But Thou art close at hand, my Lord, —
    I need not strive nor stir.

I cannot fear, and need not doubt,
    Though I be weak and low :
If Thou didst will, a mighty sword
    From out my stem should grow.

Thou hast Thy glorious forest-trees,
    Thy things of worth and power ;
But it may be Thy plan were marred
    Had I ne'er lived a flower.

Thy promise, like an evening breeze,
    Doth fold my leaves in sleep :
Who trusts, the Lord will surely guard ;
    Who loves, the Lord will keep.   SARAH WILLIAMS.

NOW IT BELONGS NOT TO MY CARE.

NOW it belongs not to my care
    Whether I die or live:
To love and serve Thee is my share,
    And this Thy grace must give.

If death shall bruise this springing seed
    Before it come to fruit,
The will with Thee goes for the deed,
    Thy life was in the root.

If life be long, I will be glad
    That I may long obey ;
If short, yet why should I be sad
    To soar to endless day ?

Christ leads me through no darker rooms
    Than he went through before ;
He that unto God's kingdom comes
    Must enter by this door.

Come, Lord, when grace hath made me meet
    Thy blessed face to see ;
For, if Thy work on earth be sweet,
    What will Thy glory be ?

My knowledge of that life is small :
    The eye of faith is dim ;
But it's enough that Christ knows all,
    And I shall be with him.   RICHARD BAXTER. 1684.

AN ACT OF FAITH IN SICKNESS.

DO I not trust in Thee, O Lord?
   Do I not rest on Thee alone?
Is not the comfort of Thy word
'The sweetest cordial I have known?
When vexed with care, bowed down with **grief**,
Where else could I obtain relief?

   And now that weakness and decay
   Forewarn me that my change draws nigh,
   Do I not feel, from day to day,
   Thou lookest down with pitying eye?
Do I not hear a still, small voice,
Bidding me still in hope rejoice?

   To Thee my inmost spirit clings:
   Like the poor dove that left the ark,
   When I forsake Thy sheltering wings,
   I meet a waste of waters dark:
Then back I fly, and grace implore
Never to wander from Thee more.

   And now on Thee I cast my soul:
   Come life or death, come ease or pain,
   Thy presence can each fear control,
   Thy grace can to the end sustain:
Those whom Thou lovest, heavenly Friend,
Thou lovest even to the end.

CHARLOTTE ELLIOTT.

HYMN FOR THE SICK.

" I will show him how great things he must suffer for my name's sake."

THY servants militant below
   Have each, O Lord, their post:
As Thou appoint'st, who best dost know
   The soldiers of Thine host:
Some in the van Thou call'st to *do*,
   And the day's heat to share;
And in the rearward not a few
   Thou only bidd'st to *bear*.

A brighter crown, perchance, is theirs,
   To the mid battle sent:
But he Thy glory also shares,
   Who waits beside* the tent.
More bravely done, in human eyes,
   The foremost post to take;
My Saviour will not those despise
   That suffer for His sake.

More honored others, Lord, may be,
   But keep me near Thy throne;
Light in Thy Light content to see,
   And never in mine own;
To keep their goal and mine in view,
   Delighted to sit still,
And evermore, if not to do,
   At least to bear, Thy Will.　　JOHN MASON NEALE

* 1 Sam. xxx. 24, 25.

SABBATH SONNET.

HOW many blessèd groups this hour are bending,
   Through   England's   primrose   meadow   paths,
   their way,
Towards spire and tower, 'midst shadowy elms ascending,
Whence the sweet chimes proclaim the hallowed day!
The halls, from old heroic ages gray,
Pour their fair children forth ; and hamlets low,
With whose thick orchard-blooms the soft winds play,
Send out their inmates in a happy flow,
Like a freed vernal stream.   I may not tread
With them those pathways, — to the feverish bed
Of sickness bound ; yet, O my God! I bless
Thy mercy, that with Sabbath peace hath filled
My chastened heart, and all its throbbings stilled
To one deep calm of lowliest thankfulness !

FELICIA D. HEMANS.
Composed a few days before her death.

MINISTERING ANGELS.

BROTHER, the angels say,
   Peace to thy heart !
We too, O brother, have
   Been as thou art, —
Hope-lifted, doubt-depressed,
   Seeing in part ;

Tried, troubled, tempted,
  Sustained, as thou art.

Brother, they softly say,
  Be our thoughts one ;
Bend thou with us and pray,
  " Thy will be done ! "
Our God is thy God ;
  He willeth the best ;
Trust Him as we trusted ;
  Rest as we rest !

Ye, too, they gently say,
  Shall angels be ;
Ye, too, O brothers,
  From earth shall be free :
Yet in earth's loved ones
  Ye still shall have part,
Bearing God's strength and love
  To the torn heart.

Thus when the spirit, tried,
  Tempted, and worn,
Finding no earthly aid,
  Heavenward doth turn,
Come these sweet angel-tones,
  Falling like balm,
And on the troubled heart
  Steals a deep calm.

HYMNS OF THE SPIRIT.

17

REJOICING IN TRIBULATION.

WHEN summer suns their radiance fling
    O'er every bright and beauteous thing;
When, strong in faith, the evil day
Of pain and grief seems far away;
When sorrow, soon as felt, is gone,
And smooth the stream of life glides on;
When duty, cheerful, chosen, free,
Brings her own prompt reward to thee;—
'Tis easy, *then*, my soul, to raise
The grateful song of heavenly PRAISE.

But, worn and languid, day and night
To see the same unchanging sight,
To feel the rising morn can bring
Nor health nor ease upon its wing,
Nor form of beauty can create,
The languid sense to renovate;
To look within, and feel the mind
Full charged with blessings for mankind;
Then, gazing round this little room,
To whisper, " This must be thy doom;
Here must thou struggle; here, alone,
Repress tired nature's rising moan:"
Oh then, my soul, how hard to raise,
In such an hour, the song of PRAISE !

To look on all this scene of tears,
Of doubts, of wishes, hopes, and fears,
As some preluding strain that tries
Our discords and our harmonies ;
To think how many a jarring string
The Master-hand in tune may bring ;
How, "finely-touched," the soul of pride
May sink, subdued and rectified ;
How, taught its inmost self to know,
May bless the hand which gave the blow —
Each root of bitterness removed,
Each plant of heavenly grace improved ; —
Instructed thus, who would not raise
To Heaven his song of cheerful PRAISE ?

To feel declining, day by day,
Each harsher murmur die away,
And secret springs of joy arise,
To lighten up the weary eyes ;
A hand invisible to feel,
Wounding, with kind design to heal,
In every bitter draught to think
Of Him who learned that cup to drink ;
Again and oft again to look
In rapture on that blessèd book,
Whose soothing words proclaim to thee
That "as thy day thy strength shall be ; "
Then, with changed heart and steadfast mind,
High Heaven before, and earth behind.

Thy path of pain again to tread,
Till earth receives thy wearied head, —
Oh blessèd lot! who would not raise,
In life or death, the song of PRAISE?

EMILY TAYLOR.

I WOULD BE THINE.

LIVING or dying, Lord, I would be Thine!
　　Oh what is life!
　　A toil, a strife,
Were it not lighted by Thy love divine.
　　I ask not wealth,
　　I crave not health; —
Living or dying, Lord, I would be Thine!

Living or dying, Lord, I would be Thine!
　　Oh what is death,
　　When the poor breath
In parting can the soul to Thee resign?
　　While patient love
　　Her trust doth prove; —
Living or dying, Lord, I would be Thine!

Living or dying, Lord, I would be Thine!
　　Throughout my days
　　Be constant praise
Uplift to Thee from out this heart of mine;
　　So shall I be
　　Brought nearer Thee, —
Living or dying, Lord, I would be Thine!

Paraphrased from FÉNÉLON; by SARAH F. ADAMS. 1841.

REST.

IT was Thy will, my Father,
   That laid Thy servant low;
It was Thy hand, my Father,
   That dealt the chastening blow;
It was Thy mercy bid me rest
   My weary soul awhile,
And every blessing I receive
   Reflects Thy gracious smile.

It is Thy care, my Father,
   That cherishes me now;
It is Thy peace, my Father,
   That rests upon my brow;
It is Thy truth, Thy truth alone,
   That gives my spirit rest,
And soothes me like a happy child
   Upon its mother's breast.

I have known youth, my Father,
   Bright as a summer's day,
And earthly love, my Father,
   But that too passed away;
Now life's small taper faintly burns,
   A little flickering flame,
But Thine eternal love remains
   Unchangeably the same.

EUPHEMIA SAXBY.

SOON — AND FOR EVER.

"SOON — and for ever!"
    Such promise our trust,
Though ashes to ashes,
    And dust unto dust.
Soon — and for ever
    Our union shall be
Made perfect, our glorious
    Redeemer, in Thee.
When the sins and the sorrows
    Of time shall be o'er;
Its pangs and its partings
    Remembered no more;
When life cannot fail,
    And when death cannot sever,
Christians with Christ shall be
    Soon — and for ever.

Soon — and for ever
    The breaking of day,
Shall drive all the night-clouds
    Of sorrow away.
Soon — and for ever
    We'll see as we 're seen,
And learn the deep meaning,
    Of things that have been.

When fightings without us,
   And fears from within,
Shall weary no more
   In the warfare of sin ;
Where tears, and where fears,
   And where death shall be — never,
Christians with Christ shall be
   Soon — and for ever.

Soon — and for ever
   The work shall be done,
The warfare accomplished,
   The victory won.
Soon — and for ever
   The soldier lay down
His sword for a harp,
   And his cross for a crown.
Then droop not in sorrow,
   Despond not in fear,
A glorious to-morrow
   Is brightening and near ;
When, blessèd reward
   Of each faithful endeavor,
Christians with Christ shall be
   Soon — and for ever.

"Her dying words to her husband were, ' Soon — and for ever.' " — *Manuscript letter.*

J. S. B. MONSELL.

VESPERS.

WHEN I have said my quiet say,
    When I have sung my little song,
How sweetly, sweetly dies the day,
The valley and the hill along ;
How sweet the summons, " Come away,"
That calls me from the busy throng !

I thought beside the water's flow
Awhile to lie beneath the leaves,
I thought in Autumn's harvest glow
To rest my head upon the sheaves ;
But lo ! methinks the day was brief
And cloudy ; flower, nor fruit, nor leaf
I bring, and yet accepted, free
And blest, my Lord, I come to Thee.

What matter now for promise lost,
Through blast of spring or summer rains !
What matter now for purpose crost,
For broken hopes and wasted pains !
What if the olive little yields !
What if the grape be blighted ! Thine
The corn upon a thousand fields,
Upon a thousand hills the vine.

My spirit bare before Thee stands :
I bring no gift, I ask no sign,
I come to Thee with empty hands,
The surer to be filled from Thine !

DORA GREENWELL.

The Last Hour.

———◦◦◦———

THE MYSTERY OF LIFE.

" Yea, though I walk through the valley of the shadow of death, I will fear no evil; for Thou art with me."

SLOWLY — slowly — darkening,
  The evening hours roll on ;
And soon behind the cloud-land
  Will sink my setting sun.

Around my path life's mysteries
  Their deepening shadows throw ;
And as I gaze and ponder,
  They dark and darker grow.

Yet still, amid the darkness,
  I feel the light is near ;
And in the awful silence
  God's voice I seem to hear : —

But I hear it as the thunder,
  Or the murmuring of the sea ;
The secret it is telling, —
  But it tells it not to me.

Yet hark ! a voice above me,
   Which says, " Wait, trust, and pray :
The night will soon be over ;
   And light will come with day."

Amen ! the light and darkness
   Are both alike to Thee :
Then to Thy waiting servant
   Alike they both shall be.

That great, unending future !
   I cannot pierce its shroud ;
But I nothing doubt, nor tremble :
   God's bow is on the cloud.

To Him I yield my spirit ;
   On Him I lay my load :
Fear ends with death ; beyond it
   I nothing see but God.

Thus moving towards the darkness,
   I calmly wait His call ;
Seeing — fearing — nothing ;
   Hoping — trusting — ALL !

SAMUEL GREG. 1868.

ABIDE WITH ME.

ABIDE with me! fast falls the even-tide:
 The darkness deepens; Lord, with me abide!
When other helpers fail, and comforts flee,
Help of the helpless, oh, abide with me!

Swift to its close ebbs out life's little day;
Earth's joys grow dim; its glories pass away;
Change and decay in all around I see:
O Thou, who changest not, abide with me!

I need Thy presence every passing hour;
What but Thy grace can foil the tempter's power?
Who like Thyself my guide and stay can be?
Through cloud and sunshine, oh, abide with me!

I fear no foe, with Thee at hand to bless:
Ills have no weight, and tears no bitterness:
Where is death's sting? where, grave, thy victory?
I triumph still, if Thou abide with me!

Hold, then, Thy cross before my closing eyes!
Shine through the gloom, and point me to the skies!
Heaven's morning breaks, and earth's vain shadows flee:
In life and death, O Lord, abide with me!

HENRY F. LYTE. 1847.

A DYING HYMN.

EARTH, with its dark and dreadful ills,
   Recedes and fades away;
Lift up your heads, ye heavenly hills;
   Ye gates of death, give way!

My soul is full of whispered song;
   My blindness is my sight;
The shadows that I feared so long
   Are all alive with light.

The while my pulses faintly beat,
   My faith doth so abound,
I feel grow firm beneath my feet
   The green immortal ground.

That faith to me a courage gives,
   Low as the grave to go;
I know that my Redeemer lives, —
   That I shall live I know.

The palace walls I almost see
   Where dwells my Lord and King;
O grave! where is thy victory?
   O death! where is thy sting?

                      ALICE CARY

THE DAY IS DONE.

THE day is done:
   Soft as a dream the sunset fades and dies,
And silent stars amid the dusky skies
   Shine one by one.

The shadows wait:
And, climbing upward over spires and towers,
Seem drawing softly this dull earth of ours
   To heaven's gate.

We wait the night
With no vain thought of darkness or of dread,
But dreams of peace for weary heart and head,
   And slumbers light.

We wait, nor fear
The few short hours of silence and of gloom
Before the eastern hills shall blush with bloom
   And morn be near.

. . . .

My God! my all!
When the dim hour grows near us by Thy grace
To meet Thy white death-angels face to face
   And hear Thy call;

When life lies low —
A gasping shadow by the altar stairs
That leadeth up from darkness unawares
   To heaven's glow;

Then let us wait
In faith and trust with prayers and blessings fond —
All mindful of the morning light beyond —
     Before the gate.

Not sore distrest,
But calmly folding life's dull garb away
Lie down in peace to wait the coming day
     And find our rest.

                   ANONYMOUS.

THE NEW HEAVEN.

LET whosoever will, inquire
     Of spirit or of seer,
To shape unto the heart's desire
The new life's vision clear.

My God, I rather look to Thee
Than to these fancies fond,
And wait till Thou reveal to me
That fair and far beyond.

I seek not of Thy Eden-land
The forms and hues to know, —
What trees in mystic order stand,
What strange, sweet waters flow ;

What duties fill the heavenly day,
Or converse glad and kind,
Or how along each shining way
The bright processions wind.

Oh, joy! to hear with sense new born
The angels' greeting strains,
And sweet to see the first fair morn
Gild the celestial plains.

But sweeter far to trust in Thee
While all is yet unknown,
And through the death-dark cheerily
To walk with Thee alone.

In Thee, my powers, my treasures live,
To Thee, my life must tend;
Giving Thyself, Thou all dost give,
O soul-sufficing friend!

And wherefore should I seek above
Thy City in the sky?
Since firm in faith, and deep in love,
Its broad foundations lie?

Since in a life of peace and prayer,
Nor known on earth, nor praised,
By humblest toil, by ceaseless care,
Its holy towers are raised.

Where faith the soul hath purified,
And penitence hath shriven,
And truth is crowned and glorified,
There — only there — is Heaven.

ELIZA SCUDDER. 1855

THE GOD OF THE LIVING.

GOD of the living, in whose eyes
　　Unveiled Thy whole creation lies !
All souls are Thine ; we must not say
That those are dead who pass away ;
From this our world of flesh set free,
We know them living unto Thee.

Released from earthly toil and strife,
With Thee is hidden still their life ;
Thine are their thoughts, their words, their powers,
All Thine, and yet most truly ours ;
For well we know, where'er they be,
Our dead are living unto Thee.

Not spilt like water on the ground,
Not wrapt in dreamless sleep profound,
Not wandering in unknown despair
Beyond Thy voice, Thine arm, Thy care ;
Not left to lie like fallen tree ;
Not dead, but living unto Thee.

O Breather into man of breath,
O Holder of the keys of death,
O Giver of the life within,
Save us from death, the death of sin,
That body, soul, and spirit be
For ever living unto Thee !

JOHN ELLERTON. 1867.

SONG FROM SINTRAM.

WHEN death is drawing near,
 And thy heart shrinks in fear,
And thy limbs fail ;
Then lift thy hands and pray
To Him who smooths the way
 Through the dark vale.

Seest thou the eastern dawn ?
Hearest thou in the red morn
 The angels' song ?
Oh ! lift thy drooping head,
Thou who in gloom and dread
 Hast lain so long.

Death comes to set thee free,
Oh, meet him cheerily
 As thy true friend !
And all thy fears shall cease,
And in eternal peace
 Thy trial end.

DE LA MOTHE FOUQUE.

AT NOONTIDE CAME A VOICE.

AT noontide came a voice, "Thou must away ;
 Hast thou some look to give, some word to say,
Or hear, of fond farewell ?" — I answered, "Nay.

18

" My soul hath said its farewell long ago ;
How light, when Summer comes, the loosened snow
Slides from the hills ! yet tell me, *where I go,*

" *Doth any wait for me ?* " Then like the clear,
Full drops of summer rain, that seem to cheer
The skies they fall from, soft within mine ear,

And slow, as if to render through that sweet
Delay a blest assurance more complete,
" Yea," only " yea," was whispered me, and then
A silence that was unto it, Amen.

" Doth any love me there," I said, "or mark
Within the dull, cold flint the fiery spark
One moment flashing out into the dark ?

" My spirit glowed, yet burned not to a clear,
Warm, steadfast flame, to lighten or to cheer."
The sweet voice said, " By things which do appear

" We judge amiss.   The flower which wears its way
Through stony chinks, lives on from day to day,
Approved for living, let the rest be gay

" And sweet as Summer ! Heaven within the reed
Lists for the flute-note, in the folded seed
It sees the bud, and in the Will the Deed."

DORA GREENWELL.

THE SOUL'S PARTING.

SHE sat within Life's Banquet Hall at noon,
  When word was brought unto her secretly :
"The Master cometh onwards quickly ; soon
Across the threshold He will call for thee."
Then she rose up to meet Him at the door,
But turning, courteous, made a farewell brief
To those that sat around.   From Care and Grief
She parted first : " Companions sworn and true
Have ye been ever to me ; but for friends
I knew ye not till later, and did miss
Much solace through that error ; let this kiss,
Late known and prized, be taken for amends.
Thou, too, kind, constant Patience, with thy slow,
Sweet counsels aiding me ; I did not know
That ye were angels, until ye displayed
Your wings for flight ; now bless me ! " but they said,
" We blest thee long ago."

Then turning unto twain
That stood together, tenderly and oft
She kissed them on their foreheads, whispering soft :
" Now must we part ; yet leave me not before
Ye see me enter safe within the Door ;
Kind bosom-comforters, that by my side
The darkest hour found ever closest bide ;

A dark hour waits me, ere for evermore
Night with its heaviness be overpast;
Stay with me till I cross the Threshold o'er."
So Faith and Hope stayed by her to the last.

But giving both her hands
To one that stood the nearest: " Thou and I
May pass together; for the holy bands
God knits on earth are never loosed on high.
Long have I walked with Thee; Thy name arose
E'en in my sleep, and sweeter than the close
Of music was Thy voice; for Thou wert sent
To lead me homewards from my banishment
By devious ways; and never hath my heart
Swerved from Thee, though our hands were wrung apart
By spirits sworn to sever us; above
Soon shall I look upon Thee as Thou art."
So she crossed o'er with Love.

DORA GREENWELL.

EPITAPH ON AN OLD MAID.

REST, gentle traveller, on life's toilsome way;
Pause here awhile; yet o'er this slumbering clay
No weeping, but a joyful tribute pay.

For this green nook, by sun and showers made warm,
Gives welcome rest to an o'erwearied form,
Whose mortal life knew many a wintry storm.

Yet, ere the spirit gained a full release
From earth, she had attained that land of peace
Where seldom clouds obscure, and tempests cease.

No chosen spot of ground she called her own ;
In pilgrim guise o'er earth she wandered on ;
Yet always in her path some flowers were strown.

No dear ones were her own peculiar care,
So was her bounty free as heaven's air ;
For every claim she had enough to spare.

And loving more her heart to give than lend,
Though oft deceived in many a trusted friend,
She hoped, believed, and trusted to the end.

She had her joys : 'twas joy to live, to love,
To labor in the world with God above,
And tender hearts that ever near did move.

She had her griefs ; but why recount them here, —
The heartsick loneness, the onlooking fear,
The days of desolation, dark and drear, —

Since every agony left peace behind,
And healing came on every stormy wind,
And still with silver every cloud was lined.

And every loss sublimed some low desire,
And every sorrow helped her to aspire,
Till waiting angels bade her go up higher !

ELIZA SCUDDER.

IN MEMORIAM.

F. D. B.

TO pass through life beloved as few are loved,
    To prove the joys of earth as few have proved,
And still to keep the soul's white robe unstained,
Such is the victory which thou hast gained.

How few like thine, the pilgrim feet that come
Unworn, unwounded, to the heavenly home !
Yet He who guides in sorrow's sorest need,
As well by pleasant paths His own may lead.

And love, that guards where wintry tempests beat,
To thee was shelter from the summer heat.   .
What need for grief to blight, or cares annoy,
The heart whose God was her exceeding joy ?

And so that radiant path, all sweet and pure,
Found fitting close in perfect peace secure ;
No haste to go, no anxious wish to stay,
No childish terror of the untried way.

But wrapped in trance of holy thought and prayer,
Yet full of human tenderness and care,
Undimmed its lustre and unchilled its love,
Thy spirit passed to cloudless light above.

In the far North, where, over frosts and gloom,
The midnight skies with rosy brightness bloom,
There comes in all the year one day complete,
Wherein the sunset and the sunrise meet.

So, in the region of thy fearless faith,
No hour of darkness marked the approach of death ;
But, ere the evening splendor was withdrawn,
Fair flushed the light along the hills of dawn.

ELIZA SCUDDER.   Dec. 4, 1871.

AH, WELL! SHE HAD HER WILL.

AH, well ! she had her will,
    Though not as she decreed it.   God saw best
To plant the warfare in her own poor breast,
To make herself her hardest, bitterest ill.
Hers was a battle where no mortal eye
    Beamed courage, and no voice cried, " Well ! "
But in the view of angel companies
        She rose and fell.

She seemed not great, nor good.
    She stood, her little space, amid the world :
    A soldier, with a banner half unfurled,
A pure high nature half misunderstood.
She loved, yet none clung closely to her side ;
    She lived, yet scarcely seemed to help a child.
Few shed a tear of sorrow when she died ;
        The angels smiled.

VOICES OF COMFORT.

OUT OF THE SHADOW.

Rejoice ye, and be glad with her, all ye that love her; rejoice for joy with her, all ye that mourn for her. — ISA. lxvi. 10.

GENTLE friends who gather here,
Drop no unavailing tear,
With no gloom surround this bier.

Bid this weary frame oppressed
Welcome to its longed-for rest
On the fair earth's sheltering breast.

And the spirit freed from clay
Give glad leave to soar away,
Singing, to the eternal day.

When this sentient life began,
Love of Nature, love of man,
Through its kindling pulses ran;

Eagerly these eyes looked forth,
Questioning the teeming earth
For its stores of truth and worth;

Head and heart with schemes were rife,
Longing for some noble strife,
Planning for some perfect life.

But the Father's love decreed
Other work and other meed,
And by ways unsought did lead ;

Turned aside the out-stretched hand,
Bade the feet inactive stand,
Checked the task that thought had planned ;

And on eyes that loved to gaze
Upon light's intensest rays
Dropped a veil of gentle haze.

How the musing spirit burned !
How the wilful nature yearned,
And its sacred limits spurned !

Known, O Father, unto Thee
All the long captivity
Of the soul at last set free ;

And how hard it was to see
Thy great harvests silently
Whitening upon land and lea ;

And to watch the reapers' throng,
Filling all the vales with song,
As they bore their sheaves along.

And to Thee, O pitying God,
Known Thy grace that overflowed
All that still and sacred road,

Where Thy patience brought relief,
Following in Thy path of grief,
Thou of suffering souls the chief !

Yet since Thou hast stooped to say,
" Cast thy out-worn robe away,
Come and rest with me to-day, —

" Come to larger life and power,
Come to strength renewed each hour,
Come to truth's unfailing dower ; — "

To the dear ones gathered here
Make Thy loving purpose clear,
And Thy light shine round this bier.

ELIZA SCUDDER. 1872.

AFTER DEATH IN ARABIA.

HE who died at Azan sends
    This to comfort all his friends :

Faithful friends !   It lies, I know,
Pale and white and cold as snow ;
And ye say, " Abdallah 's dead ! "
Weeping at the feet and head,
I can see your falling tears,
I can hear your sighs and prayers ;

Yet I smile and whisper this, —
" *I* am not the thing you kiss ;
Cease your tears, and let it lie ;
It *was* mine ; it is not I."

Sweet friends !   What the women lave
For its last bed of the grave,
Is but a hut which I am quitting,
Is a garment no more fitting,
Is a cage from which, at last,
Like a hawk my soul has passed.
Love the inmate, not the room, —
The wearer, not the garb, — the plume
Of the falcon, not the bars
Which kept him from those splendid stars.

Loving friends !   Be wise and dry
Straightway every weeping eye, —
What ye lift upon the bier
Is not worth a wistful tear.
'Tis an empty sea-shell, — one
Out of which the pearl is gone ;
The shell is broken, it lies there ;
The pearl, the all, the soul, is here.
'Tis an earthen jar, whose lid
Allah sealed, the while it hid
That treasure of his treasury,
A mind that loved him ; let it lie !
Let the shard be earth's once more,
Since the gold shines in his store.

Allah glorious !   Allah good !
Now the world is understood ;
Now the long, long wonder ends ;
Yet ye weep, my erring friends,
While the man whom ye call dead,
In unspoken bliss, instead,
Lives and loves you ; lost, 'tis true,
By such light as shines for you ;
But, in the light ye cannot see
Of unfulfilled felicity, —
In enlarging Paradise, —
Lives a life that never dies.

Farewell, friends !   Yet not farewell ;
Where I am, ye, too, shall dwell.
I am gone before your face,
A moment's time, a little space.
When ye come where I have stepped
Ye will wonder why ye wept.
Ye will know, by wise love taught,
That here is all, and there is naught.
Weep awhile, if ye are fain, —
Sunshine still must follow rain ;
Only not at death, — for death,
Now I know, is that first breath
Which our souls draw when we enter
Life, which is of all life centre.

Be ye certain, all seems love,
Viewed from Allah's throne above ;
Be ye stout of heart, and come
Bravely onward to your home !
La Allah illa Allah !   Yea !
Thou love divine ! Thou love alway !

He that died at Azan gave
This to those who made his grave.

EDWIN ARNOLD, from the Arabic.

IN MEMORIAM.

FAREWELL ! since nevermore for thee
    The sun comes up our eastern skies,
Less bright henceforth shall sunshine be
· To some fond hearts and saddened eyes.

There are, who for thy last, long sleep,
    Shall sleep as sweetly nevermore ;
Shall weep because thou canst not weep,
    And grieve that all thy griefs are o'er.

Sad thrift of love ! the loving breast
    On which thine aching head was thrown
Gave up the weary head to rest,
    But kept the aching for its own.

R. J.   1867.

THE CONQUEROR'S GRAVE.

WITHIN this lowly grave a Conqueror lies,
　　And yet the monument proclaims it not,
Nor round the sleeper's name hath chisel wrought
The emblems of a fame that never dies, —
　　Ivy and amaranth, in a graceful sheaf,
　　Twined with the laurel's fair imperial leaf.
　　　　A simple name alone,
　　　　To the great world unknown,
Is graven here, and wild-flowers rising round,
Meek meadow-sweet, and violets of the ground,
　　　　Lean lovingly against the humble stone.

Here, in the quiet earth, they laid apart
　　No man of iron mould and bloody hands,
　　Who sought to wreak upon the cowering lands
The passions that consumed his restless heart ;
　　But one of tender spirit and delicate frame,
　　　　Gentlest, in mien and mind,
　　　　Of gentle womankind,
　　Timidly shrinking from the breath of blame ;
One in whose eyes the smile of kindness made
　　Its haunt, like flowers by sunny brooks in May,
Yet, at the thought of others' pain, a shade
　　Of sweeter sadness chased the smile away.

Nor deem that when the hand that moulders here
Was raised in menace, realms were chilled with fear,

And armies mustered at the sign, as when
Clouds rise on clouds before the rainy East, —
  Gray captains leading bands of veteran men
And fiery youths to be the vulture's feast.
Not thus were waged the mighty wars that gave
The victory to her who fills this grave :
        Alone her task was wrought,
        Alone the battle fought ;
Through that long strife her constant hope was staid
On God alone, nor looked for other aid.

She met the hosts of Sorrow with a look
  That altered not beneath the frown they wore,
And soon the lowering brood were tamed, and took,
  Meekly, her gentle rule, and frowned no more.
Her soft hand put aside the assaults of wrath,
        And calmly broke in twain
        The fiery shafts of pain,
And rent the nets of passion from her path.
  By that victorious hand despair was slain ;
With love she vanquished hate, and overcame
  Evil with good, in her great Master's name.

Her glory is not of this shadowy state,
  Glory that with the fleeting season dies ;
But, when she entered at the sapphire gate,
  What joy was radiant in celestial eyes !
How heaven's bright depths with sounding welcomes
        rung,

And flowers of heaven by shining hands were flung!
   And He who, long before,
   Pain, scorn, and sorrow bore,
The Mighty Sufferer, with aspect sweet,
Smiled on the timid stranger from his seat;
He who returning, glorious, from the grave,
Dragged Death, disarmed, in chains, a crouching slave.

See, as I linger here, the sun grows low;
 Cool airs are murmuring that the night is near.
O gentle sleeper, from thy grave I go,
 Consoled though sad, in hope and yet in fear.
   Brief is the time, I know,
   The warfare scarce begun;
Yet all may win the triumphs thou hast won.
Still flows the fount whose waters strengthened thee;
 The victors' names are yet too few to fill
Heaven's mighty roll; the glorious armory,
 That ministered to thee, is open still.
      WILLIAM C. BRYANT.

IN MEMORY

OF THE LADY AUGUSTA STANLEY.

"Ye shall indeed drink of the cup that I drink of."
"They serve Him day and night."

OH, blessed life of service and of love!
 Heart wide as life, deep as life's deepest woe;
His servants serve Him day and night above.
 Thou servedst day and night, we thought, below.

Hands full of blessings lavished far and wide,
   Hands tender to bind up hearts wounded sore ;
Stooping quite down earth's lowest needs beside, —
   Master, like Thee! we thought, and said no more.

  .   .   .   .

Oh, nerves and heart racked to their utmost strain ;
   Hands stretched in helplessness to serve no more ;
Dulled by no slumber to thy deepest pain, —
   Master, like Thee! we wept, and said no more.

We o'er all sorrow would have raised thee up,
   Crowned with life's choicest blossoms night and morn ;
God made thee drink of His Beloved's cup,
   And crowned thee with the Master's crown of thorn.

Looking from thee to Him once wounded sore,
   We learned a little more His face to see ;
Then, looking from the cross for us He bore,
   To thine, we almost understood for thee !

Till now, again ! we gaze on thee above,
   Strong and unwearied, serving day and night ;
Oh, blessed life of service and of love !
   Master, like Thee, and with Thee, in Thy light !

ELIZABETH CHARLES.
March 9, 1876.

THE RETURN HOME.

SAFE home, safe home in port!
    Rent cordage, shattered deck,
Torn sails, provisions short,
    And only not a wreck:
But oh the joy upon the shore,
To tell our voyage-perils o'er!

The prize, the prize secure!
    The athlete nearly fell;
Bare all he *could* endure,
    And bare not always well:
But he may smile at troubles gone
Who sets the victor-garland on!

No more the foe can harm;
    No more of leaguered camp,
And cry of night-alarm,
    And need of ready lamp:
And yet how nearly he had failed, —
How nearly had that foe prevailed!

St. Joseph of the Studium. a.d. 870.
Tr. by J. Mason Neale.

HYMN SUNG AT A FUNERAL.

COME forth! come on, with solemn song!
    The road is short, the rest is long!
The Lord brought here, He calls away:
    Make no delay,
This home was for a passing day.

Here in an inn a stranger dwelt,
Here joy and grief by turns he felt;
Poor dwelling, now we close thy door!
    The task is o'er,
The sojourner returns no more!

Now of a lasting home possest,
He goes to seek a deeper rest.
Good night! the day was sultry here,
    In toil and fear,
Good night! the night is cool and clear.

F. SACHSE.

Index of Titles.

Index of Authors.

Index of First Lines.

QUIET HOURS.

A COLLECTION OF POEMS, MEDITATIVE AND RELIGIOUS.

FIRST AND SECOND SERIES.

" Such a book as this seems to us much better adapted than any formal book of devotion to beget a calm and prayerful spirit in the reader. It will no doubt become a dear companion to many earnestly religious people." — *Christian Register.*

"Thousands of thoughtful and devout minds have been helped, comforted, and strengthened by the little volume of poetical selections, published under the title of ' Quiet Hours,' some years since ; and these and many more will welcome a new volume, published under the same title, constructed on the same plan, and breathing the same earnest and gentle spirit. This second series of ' Quiet Hours,' like the first, bears the imprint of Roberts Bros. It is contained in a dainty little volume of the Little Classic style, prettily printed and bound ; and there are not far from two hundred pieces in it, grouped under the heads, ' Nature,' 'Morning and Evening,' ' Inward Strife,' ' Life and Duty,' ' Prayer and Aspiration,' ' Trust and Adoration,' ' Heaven and the Saints,' and ' Miscellaneous.' The poems are chosen with exquisite taste ; their range is broad, and their tone is clear and true." — *Boston Journal.*

" 'Quiet Hours' is the appropriate title which some unnamed compiler has given to a collection of musings of many writers, — a nosegay made up of some slighter, choicer, and more delicate flowers from the garden of the poets. Emerson, Chadwick, Higginson, Arnold, Whittier, and Clough are represented, as well as Coleridge, Browning, Wordsworth, and Tennyson ; and the selections widely vary in character, ranging from such as relate to the moods and aspects of nature, to voices of the soul when most deeply stirred." — *Congregationalist.*

18mo, cloth, red edges. **Price,** $1.00 each. Two vols. in one. **Price, $1**.50 ; calf or seal, $4.00. Sold by all booksellers. Mailed **post-paid,** by the Publishers,

ROBERTS BROTHERS,

BOSTON.

SUNSHINE IN THE SOUL.

POEMS *SELECTED* BY THE EDITOR OF "QUIET HOURS."

———◆———

"Another delicate little *morceau* of a book. Seemly in its outer garb, but incomparably more beautiful within. A cunningly selected group, by the hand of a skilful arranger of poems, from the choicest writers. An exquisite and precious little book, that will doubtless let God's sunshine into many a sad soul." — *Christian Intelligencer.*

"'Sunshine in the Soul' is a collection, in a bijou volume, of a number of the most beautiful, tender, uplifting, and satisfying verses of a religious character which exist in our language. There is abundance of help and comfort in this little volume, and many a heart will be made glad in its possession." — *Boston Traveller.*

"Designed, as its title indicates, to cheer and elevate, and to be a bright companion for the reader. It is pleasant to find such a book of religious verse, that has nothing austere or gloomy in its pages, nothing that seems to darken heaven to man." — *Portland Press.*

———◆———

First and Second Series, 18mo, cloth. Price, 50 cents each. Both series in one volume, price 75 cents. Sold by all Booksellers. Mailed, postpaid, by the Publishers,

ROBERTS BROTHERS,

Boston

THE "WISDOM SERIES."

EDITED BY THE EDITOR OF "QUIET HOURS" AND "SURSUM CORDA."

" These little volumes, small enough for the pocket, and neat enough for the cabinet or parlor table, are admirably selected from two of the books which can never grow old nor lose their charm to devout and meditative minds. They may well lead the 'Wisdom Series.' The editor who gave us the excellent volume of selected poems called 'Quiet Hours,' and who has just prepared another and similar book, has done the public a service by here putting together in compact form the best of the thoughts and aspirations which this generation is too little disposed to look for amidst the less pregnant and valuable matter with which they are mingled in the full editions. A brief, but compact and readable, memoir prefaces each volume." — *Unitarian Review.*

SELECTIONS FROM THE IMITATION OF CHRIST. By Thomas à Kempis.

SELECTIONS FROM THE THOUGHTS OF MARCUS AURELIUS ANTONINUS.

SUNSHINE IN THE SOUL. Poems selected by the Editor of " Quiet Hours." First Series.

SUNSHINE IN THE SOUL. Second Series.

SELECTIONS FROM EPICTETUS.

THE WISDOM OF JESUS, THE SON OF SIRACH ; OR, ECCLESIASTICUS.

THE WISDOM OF SOLOMON, AND OTHER SELECTIONS FROM THE APOCRYPHA.

SELECTIONS FROM FÉNELON.

THE LIFE AND SERMONS OF THE REVEREND DOCTOR JOHN TAULER.

SOCRATES, THE APOLOGY AND CRITO OF PLATO.

SOCRATES, THE PHÆDO OF PLATO.

18mo, cloth, red edges. Price, 50 cents each. Complete sets (two vols. in one). 6 vols. in a box. Price, $4.50. Sold by all Booksellers. Mailed, post-paid, by the Publishers,

ROBERTS BROTHERS, BOSTON.